MALAGAN

AND

S
E
C
INTER
I
O
N

(First paperback edition May 2025)

ISBN 978-1-7641094-7-5 (Paperback)

Also By Rory Haymont

The Dreamer

Zen

Bruja

Kirby

Three Novellas

Proximity

The Hand of Tæranon

The Survivor

Nance

The Blue Groper

Names

The Baker's Dozen

Short Novels

The Girlfriend Experience

Reaper

The Blue Groper

Proximity

The Reputation

Short Stories

Clean

Holes

The Hostel

Death Row

Sheds

Crayons

The Dog's Dream

Revenge of the Geriatrics

The Art Piece

The Last Embrace

The Donation

Bottom Feeders

Run

MALAGAN

He approached the two Malagan as he walked along the path through the park he took to go to work. It wasn't on his way to work. In fact he had to leave half an hour early to walk that way. However there were a few plants from the 'Sacred Lands', which had established there, even though the earthlings had not cultivated them intentionally. This included a beautiful mauve grass. If he took his shoes off, when he was sure no one was looking, it was like walking through a silky pool of water. Yet his feet came away dry and feeling as good as he imagined that part of your body could feel. He'd had many such experiences. Though no one else had any idea where and when. It was the great secret of his life.

Two Malagan were sitting on a table with their boots on the bench seats. If they'd been human, he'd say they were 'chatting'. However all the dramatic 'cultural sensitivity' training they were required to do about the species, never delivered by a Malagan, but rather a breathless xenoanthropologist, suggested the Malagan were unlikely to have a 'chat'. Even amongst themselves and certainly not with a human.

No one providing any of the training could confirm this because the only interactions they had with the Malagan were fleeting observations as one of their number came to place orders for stores from the company supermarket nearest the colony. The aliens did this when the venue was closed to earthlings for the purpose. They were not subtle about their prejudices. They didn't like humans. They were considered usurpers, who, albeit peacefully, and had taken over their planet. It was a peaceful takeover because a particular human had appraised the Malagan of her species capacity and historical predilection for wholesale destruction, and suggested they should sue for peace. On earth, supporters of such a 'noble and sensible capitulation' worked hard to ensure the maintenance of the Malagan's existence untroubled by change, except for the technological and dietary improvements to their of life they grudgingly accepted. Limited within the realms of their pathological asceticism.

One of their number, apparently most unhappy to be given the onerous task of interacting with the store manager, inventoried what they wanted delivered to the large walled communities they lived in. With no payment required and with never a thank you the Malagan would leave. The treaty they signed required neither.

They eschewed such a decadent device as a phone to simply call in their list. They acquired nothing in the way of entertainment nor sources of information which would in any way enlighten them with respect to human nature, history or any information regarding the earthlings homeland. The Malagan's view was that they had their own trove of knowledge and polluting it with anything human was another, on a long list, of things they did not do.

This included human food which they found disgusting. In their rare exchanges this was one of the first topics of conversation. It smelled, tasted and looked vile. Humans could never repay the compliment in kind because they were never offered anything to eat. The one exception was the superior nature of human bread. However, rather than procure flour which could have been provided in large qualities, they acquired wheat seed so they could grow the plants and grind the seed into an inferior flour and make a poor quality, unleavened bread. Still better however than that which they produced before the invasion. The 'Cultural Sensitivity' trainers found it hard to fill in even an hour. Let alone the three the company insisted on. They did this to demonstrate, not to the Malagan who didn't care, but to the company's stakeholders who wanted to assure themselves that company employees did.

After the Malagan capitulation to an AI trillionaire, negotiators were despatched from all of the hundreds of Malagan communities to assemble in a hall the humans built for the purpose as the natives had nothing to conduct such a meeting in. They were collected in sub space shuttles, their rudimentary vehicles too slow to satisfy the human lust for a timely resolution followed closely by exploitation of the resources. The Malagan had created a new piece of cultural apparel for the gathering. Veils to shield themselves from what they were sure would be the haughty gaze of the human conquerors. The humans were discomfited when they were told they wouldn't be invited to the negotiations. The Malagan wanted a week to discuss these momentous issues. They were finished by the middle of the second day. One 'negotiator' was sent out. The leader, or Bekou, of the largest community. The communities collaborated on areas where it was logical to be federal, but were fiercely independent in local affairs within what was a universally narrow interpretation of dogma. Also, in order to maintain a vibrant gene pool, they observed some rituals the objective of which was simple genetic diversity.

News had trickled out to the earthlings that the Malagan had only one gender. They could reproduce both 'sexually' or 'asexually'. The human negotiators, later, somewhat unkindly, suggested the latter methodology was likely to be much more common as they would not need to be confronted with the prospect of intimacy. This was not because the Malagan were homely. Convergent evolution had left them not so different to humans. Such views were formed based on what appeared to be intractably droll personalities now punctuated by chauvinism and occasionally a simple meanness. But humans only met the very old, who schooled the long-lived species to that mindset from youth.

The Bekou chosen to be the negotiator had gone back and forward on a few occasions. The humans as the colonists, went out of their way to accommodate what were, fortunately for all, surprisingly easy arrangements to come to.

The centrepiece of the Malagan position was that they wanted to be left alone and as little of their planet 'despoiled', as could be managed.

The humans found Malagan's views about and relationship with the land enigmatic. They lived on the borders of beautiful natural wildernesses they never visited and insisted the human never did either. The rest of the planet was a barren, mostly waterless wasteland that didn't even boast the kind of beauty a barren landscape in the sunset or sunrise might. The rising and setting of their sun were further apart with the diurnal cycle of thirty hours as the smaller planet turned more sluggishly, however it's orientation provided no seasonal variations. Most of the communities were in the equatorial regions and so there was generally fifteen hours of daylight and fifteen of darkness. Some earthlings found that adjustment impossible to cope with. Others worked eight hours a day and enjoyed sport, or hobbies or walking in the parks and domes constructed to replicate various earth environments. The company made an enormous amount of money so it could terraform large areas and create all kinds of venues and entertainments, schools and recreation centres. Some didn't want their contracts to end. Others took the next ship home after arriving.

There was more than enough mineral wealth in the barren lands to last the earthlings tens of thousands of years. It did however have to be very high grade and processed to a very high degree of purity to justify the cost of moving it around. Some humans were sceptical about the Malagan's point of view concerning the mining areas. In addition to the sacred forest, woodlands, plains and heaths, which leaked drone footage did confirm to be very beautiful though strange; the barren areas were also allegedly sacred. Both were so sacred, the Malagan never visited them.

In the borderlands they took water from the rivers that exited from the forests which eventually became contaminated prior to drying up in the wastelands. The Malagan communities were surrounded by large walls, and all situated near such a river exit, which left the more diverse sacred lands via caves under the ranges that separated the two landscapes. They had extensive gardens and orchards, but with only a fraction of the varieties their forebearers had once cultivated. Those ancient Malagan, now forgotten in the collective memory, lived on, only in writings which were known only to the Bekou and leaders of each community. The Botlu being the name for the collective of these leaders on the rare occasions the leadership met as a group. The Malagan travelled between communities, through the barren lands to fulfil a mathematically guided undertaking which was ritualised as a rite of passage.

So when Henry approached two Malagan in a park it was unusual to say the least and he looked around in case something was going on that he should be avoiding.

He came level with the pair, not sure if he should look into their eyes and say hello or pass by. The Cultural Awareness training was complete garbage as far he was concerned and prejudiced a whole species based on the behaviours of the few miserable specimens in charge. He had always believed these were a good people, pissed off at what fate had dealt them, and this hadn't brought out the best in them. He said hello to any entity he walked past. Even a dog. Then he felt bad for making such a comparison which caused him to re-evaluate the entire hello decision.

In the end it didn't matter. A face, with no emotional signals his mind was able to fathom, cast forth a greeting. 'And where are you off to on this fine morn?'

This caught him completely off guard. But he was able to bounce back easily with a simple. 'I'm going to work.'

'Ah. Work. You humans seem obsessed by it. It takes up so much of your time which might otherwise be spent with those whom you are related or make close associations.'

'I feel that way sometimes.'

'Maybe in your case those for which you have close associations and are related prefer it that you work.'

Henry's wife spent more than half her time off planet visiting their children who, only the younger had ever visited. He had begged to complete his last two years of school on earth. It took two 'experienced' weeks to get between the planets ever since the earthlings found there was a worm hole sitting quietly in the middle of nowhere about double the distance to the moon. It took one of the first Mars colonisation ships to disappear through it by accident to discover it's whereabouts. The captain was enough of a science fiction buff to decide he knew what was going on when he felt the very strange process of having his body age a little faster than usual. There was a vast pallet of unfamiliar stars he might have splashed his name over. But he was the bus driving variety of space captain not one for a voyage of exploration. It was fortunate that he stayed a little while to capture what he could of the stars using the instruments he had. If he'd turned back to earth sooner, he would have arrived before he left, or passed himself in the worm hole. This might cause an awkward sort of looping scientists would rather not contemplate. It was established that the ship had been away for an hour however it physically returned after ten minutes.

Now if one did a round trip from earth to Malagan they would only be away for five days. But the traveller's lived experience was a little under a month depending on the kind of transport.

Henry stood looking at the two beings, both leaning back casually on arms behind them. They had been quick to strike at the heart of his conundrum. He and his wife, whom he loved dearly, had seen their relationship atrophy as he continued working on the planet longer than they'd intended to. They could retire comfortably in middle age, or he could take his pick of senior corporate jobs if he wanted to work. So he decided to see theirs as an apt observation in his case rather than the kind of mean jibe those completing the cultural awareness training might expect to receive. 'In my case your analysis is a good one. But other humans are often much more closely associated, and their work is a secondary consideration.'

'I see. Unlike the Malagan who spend even more time in labour than you, and have no memory of those who spawned us, and have none of what you would call warmth or fellowship to share. It's a life of pointless drudgery. An ironic hive-bound loneliness.'

Henry looked the Malagan speaking in the eye and said. 'I don't believe you.'

The smile he received was transformative. The cultural awareness training said their faces were incapable of emotional 'signalling'.

The Malagan looked at the other. 'Just as our revered elders told us. Spend even a moment with a human and if they're not being culturally insensitive in some myriad ways for their own amusement, they'll be accusing you of falsehood after the briefest exchange.'

The other joined in. Also smiling. 'Is he a better or worse example of their kind? And does it matter?'

'As your meanspirited anthropologists and cultural trainers point out, correctly, our kind do not smile. My sister and I have trained our faces to do that for our interactions with humans. Hence, we have come here and suffered the first of what I now realise will be the beginning of many disappointments.'

Henry knew people. He could be very social but had developed solitary interests. 'Perhaps you did this for your own amusement or to discomfit humans.'

'Now he accuses us of falsehoods for no greater purpose than an infatuation with trivialities. Would that we were conquered by more understanding slave masters. It makes the native dreariness of our lives more awful to know we're so despised beyond our walls.'

The interactions between the two reminded Henry of a particular example of humanity having a conversation. He didn't reflect sufficiently before answering 'A culture of drudgery and social repression could never produce two such delightful young lad…'

It hung there. He had made what was one of the few things he believed the Cultural Awareness training to be accurate about. The She/Him or Shim issue. Those who took on the self-appointed role of pronoun generation and enforcement in society had determined that 'members of the intergalactic community' whom earthlings had 'deflowered' for the sake of corporate greed 'were to be referred to as Shims when a pronoun was required as they were at the same time and never both a 'she and a he'. Therefore: a Shim. However. This was never to be used in their presence. The self-appoint pronoun enforcers, along with everyone else on earth, didn't know if the Malagan used pronouns.

'He leads us along with only casual rudeness and indifference to our ways only so he can bring us to a place he can lash out with the most egregious insult one could make to our innocent and luckless species. Did our benighted Bekou negotiate permission to give such offence from his kind?' The slightly more serious of the two intoned.

The other shook 'her' head in sad wonder. 'He has positioned us thus my sister. To suggest our proudest attribute as a species can be disregarded and not only does he suggest we have two genders, he takes it further and insults us by assigning us one of them.'

'And in the same short sentence consigns us to infanthood.'

'I feel defiled sister. Young ladies. We might be seventy in his years. Or robust, tending towards the masculine of his species should we have any such tendencies. Which we do not. Why would we. So deeply satisfied we are in the singular.'

Henry was starting to knit his brows a little at all the 'sister' references. He wasn't sure that any contributions he made could help or clarify or achieve anything other than bring further chastisement. Now flaw was found even in his strategy to cause no further offence.

'And now he decides ignoring us is the best strategy to add to the many lacerations and bruises he has caused. Do these humans study in the time they have leisure to be ready, in the case of the smallest chance, there should be an opportunity to inflict more pain on the race they conquered. All innocent as we were of the very concept of casual meanness.'

'Who can tell sister. We can only be glad that our lives are defined by drudgery and the pointless study of useless knowledge intermixed with meaningless chants. Our worthless activities, tedious though they may be, are not oriented singularly towards hurtfulness.'

'Yes sister. And he goes further. There is no hatred. Only hurtfulness. As if our species are such poor examples of a living being we are not even worth the energy expended to hate us. Casual mockery only. Perhaps some well-practiced pretence of pity will be next. At least we can take comfort in what a venerable earthling philosopher once said. It is better to be wronged than to do wrong. Yet I fear this particular example of humanity, if he only could, would lead us into the kind of wrongness he is so well practiced at. And so he would complete our humiliation.'

They both laughed. A different laugh to the human kind without question, but one with the same quality as two sharp teenage friends or perhaps sisters being mischievous. The taller of the two got off the table. She was more than a head taller than him, yet it wasn't something she took advantage of in her stance. She reached out her hand to Henry. Smiling. The laugh and smile were unique, but the messages they sent were universal. He shook the 'Shims' hand. Relieved that he hadn't caused what, given the paucity of interaction, could have become an intergalactic incident, but more so he was pleased that his belief that the Malagan were good natured was accurate.

As he took her hand and introduced himself, it produced a strange sensation. A sensation he had felt elsewhere. But not so pure. 'We are young, what would you have said… ladies?' He nodded. He was a throwback to an earlier age. 'What should we call you. 'Old Gentleman'. I'm Semaj and this is my sister Eilarch. We heard about the gender issue and how fearful you all are of causing offence about it. We aren't typical of out species. When we learned genders existed, we decided we liked the feminine kind, and we are indeed sisters. We've maintained our sibling relationship. Contrary to the ways of the Malagan.'

Eilarch came in turn to shake hands. She was not quite as tall, and her touch held the same connection he was familiar with, flavoured a little more with a sense of fun and buoyancy, 'Indeed Old Gentleman, we two are abnormal. Our society is dull and pursues pointless study to fill long and joyless lives with an absence of individuality nor any form of intimate interaction. Just as your Xenophobic race imagines us to be. My sister and I are different.' She made a thoughtful face. Recognisable in what it conveyed to a human, though composed differently. 'I will try to recall what word the earthlings would use.'

'Eilarch their language is difficult for us. Ours being so pallid and doleful in its tiresome simplicity. I think they would label us as…freaks sister. Not a positive alternative to Malagan. Merely an acknowledgement that we have unfavourable character traits over and above those of the erstwhile heirs to the planet.'

Henry thought he'd jumped in with what was on his mind. 'Now that the whole young lady thing has been turned back on me as 'old gentleman' I can see it's…patronising.'

A dark shape appeared among the trees some distance off. 'Ah. Our mistress appears. Looking for us. Escapees from the hive where we live out our bitter lives. Misery our constant companion. And now the ill-advised time here spent with you will lead us to the Disapprobation Ritual. A punishment inflicted upon us unlooked for. All we wanted was to enjoy a brief freedom in a park. With a few stolen moments with some beautiful plants our species treats with reverential ignorance. Not expecting a human to detour so far from home to come upon us unexpected.'

Henry hoped they were continuing in their flippant narrative style when speaking of the consequences of being caught with a human. The dark presence didn't approach. It waited at a distance.

'They have enhanced the Disapprobation Ritual since you earthlings brought the 'bounty of your civilisation'. Our elders can now bond broken glass to their whips to flail our young bodies before the entire hive. A lesson to those who would consort with our slave masters.' The two looked at each other in a forlorn fashion as they turned to go. 'Henry. Though we might scream in pain as they rip and rend our young flesh, I know my sister and I feel the same. Meeting you has been the highlight of our pathetic lives. You've proven our myopic elders wrong, just as we suspected. Farewell.'

'I'll receive no ill treatment and can only hope you do not. But please believe me that meeting you has been…the highlight of my life.'

The two had been walking away when Semaj turned back. A look written on her face of one who had thought him trustworthy. But was now not so sure. 'Better than your marriage day and those days of the birth of the young you helped spawn.'

Henry said with no hesitation. 'I can tell you truly that it is.'

Semaj smiled and walked on. They came to where the old Malagan stood. This was not the one designated to come for 'supplies'. Though she did this also; in secret. The old one smiled up at them. They were two heads taller than her.

'He's the one?'

Semaj was relieved and pleased. 'He's the one.'

Henry sat at work, which could be fascinating at times and could be a pointless exercise when he and most of those around them could get the day's work done in half the time if they wanted to deliver at peak efficiency. However, there was no incentive to do so. And although retirement was possible, those he helped spawn were not quite low maintenance yet. He didn't need to be concerned that he had lied to the two Malagan about how important it had been for him to meet them. He hadn't. He was more than a little ashamed that it should be the truth. But Henry wasn't a man to lie. Even to himself. Meeting them, and then via the brief hand shake, the two had connected him more intimately to something he had been completely beguiled by.

He decided the last thing he would do is reveal the exchange, to his knowledge, the most illuminating to date with the Malagan. Partly because he suspected they were unrepresentative. Which he now thought he should have suggested was a better descriptor than freaks.

The meeting further impeded him from doing what he knew he should do. Which was to advise the company he would not be renewing his contract, take the generous long service bonus, and go back to earth. He could be with his wife full time, semi retire to a lucrative consultancy and visit his children every few days or weeks. More frequently in the case of Raven who was their favourite child. Daughter-in-law though she might be.

Henry walked through the forest parkland the next day to see the same two at the rarely used picnic table. Eirlahc sitting on the table section with feet on the bench, Semaj sitting on the bench looking away from the table with elbows behind holding herself up. If he had been British, he might observe that they were intentionally 'lolling about'. And though not looking directly at each other they were engaged in a dialogue, smiling and laughing as many a teenage girl, boy or shim might.

Like most people on earth he had been told again and again to completely ignore what he observed daily as reality. He needed to accept the constructed reality which the powerful self-appointed cabal of mind police had conceived. And should also accept they had every right to enforce everyone's belief in the reality they had constructed.

In Henry's reality, it was obvious they were feigning not to notice his approach. He took advantage of this. 'I hadn't expected to meet you both again given the trouble I caused you. It's a great pleasure for me to see you.'

Eilrahc stopped looking at the pale blue sky. Blue for the same reasons it's blue on earth; and look across at him. 'You must have seen we were only pretending to laugh and 'chat' as some of your species call it Henry. However, as you arrived, we both realised we would not be able sustain the pretence. Our poor tender bodies were lashed mercilessly. Hidden beneath these clownish coverings, completely unnecessary for hermaphrodites as mating is mechanistic in our case and the sight of one body or another has no bearing on our mathematically driven assignations. Hence, we lack agency even in our primary evolutionary function.'

'Details are whispered among our repressed community of the loathsome physical forms humans have had the ill fortune to evolve. Merely to facilitate the simple transaction of gametes. Because we are free from what we understand to be both the complex psychological and physical machinations to produce spawn, our kind has so much more time to devote to a lifetime of slavish adherence to tiresome codes and study of baleful dogma. Through this we can generate a capacity for mendacity likely to be unparallel in the universe.'

Henry wasn't sure where to start in answer to this. Perhaps some diminution of his own species. An observation as to the sometimes arduous nature of human sexuality could be crafted. He was wondering if the best answer was to honestly describe the fact there was a great deal of material to sift through when Semaj filled the space.

'He cares so little for us and our culture that he wasn't even listening sister. Even to the extent that he might, out of a pretence of courtesy, seek some small clarification or offer an insight into his culture. He perhaps wishes his pathway to work, unnecessarily trodden through this sad parody of a natural Malagan forest, was kept free of its native inhabitants. The landscape he and his kind have so mercilessly abused, should not be interrupted with our tiresome insights into our culture, hitherto shared with none.'

'I think it may be embarrassment sister. That he might be called upon to provide insights to the nature of the sexuality of his species. I mean...yeerch. Those voids and appendages which are whispered about by the less proper of our kind.'

'My guess sister, is rather than salacious facts, perhaps these impossibly horrid genitalia are mere fabrications which our elders have devised to frighten the young into immediate submission. Hence another ruse to maintain, stupid and gullible as we are, our state of crippling conformity.'

Henry thought he better jump right in to ensure them these conversations, however unusual, were something he was willing to fully, and frankly participate in.

'It is true that our approach to sexuality can cause some of the basest human behaviour...'

'Xenophobia being an example of another base behaviour.'

'Very true. We have a history of intolerance when confronted with….'

'We have no diversity. So Xenophobia used to be an impossibility for us.'

'If your reproductive approach hasn't been the source of the development of baser instincts perhaps there have been some advantages …'

'You're suggesting our lack of diversity automatically translates to narrowness of outlook. Shallowness in our capabilities to live and interact such that we…'

'No I was wanting to provide a perspective on…'

'It is unconscionably rude to interrupt someone in our culture Henry.'

'Oh I didn't realise. It's similar in our…'

'It's worse than a Malagan making irreverent references to one of our sexual appendages.'

Henry waited a little to be sure it was time for a response. He was not going to rise to the challenge of a commentary on sexual appendages. For either species. 'I may not be representative of our species. You have revealed somewhat of a bad habit on my part that I tend to inter…'

'I'm surprised that you would let it pass that I provided you with the fictitious and indeed ludicrous suggestion that we have sexual appendages at all. Of course we do not. It reveals a troubling unannounced voyeurism to allow such obvious untruths to pass by without examination.'

Henry waited again before saying. 'I have much to apologise for. Indeed I'm losing count of my failures to…' Henry was now quite enjoying himself. Scrupulous not to show it though.

Eilrahc waded in. 'It is you sister, who interrupted the earthling. Contrary to the hundreds of behavioural guidances, about this being the largest in number each day, and being close to the apex of things we do not do.'

'It's not a problem. As I say. I can be a little prone interr…'

'I've fallen into the trap of one who must study long into the night to bring us so low. To become nothing. Ashamed. Reviling of my own self. Seduced into a slightly alluring opportunity to communicate with a being from another planet. And here this example of his species has obviously prepared a contrivance that was long in the planning and careful in the delivery to leave me shunned by my own kind.

Indeed sister will you ever be able to be able to look upon me as other than a traitor to our values. A repugnant thing?'

'Is it possible we could reset the conversation? Start again.' Said Henry helpfully. 'I think there have been some misunderstandings of a cultural nature, so why not be understanding towards each other and forgive ourselves for any ...'

'Semaj, he at last offers up a pathway to the final degradation of our values. Participation in subterfuge. Devising an alluring opportunity to pretend at forgetfulness of all the many sins he's caused us to partake in. So many that we must now be unique in our species to have so trampled our culture, dull as it is, to meaningless fragments. He would convince us to be liars now. Deniers of our wrongdoing.'

'That's true sister. All we came to do is to plead with him not to mention our last meeting and that he should share none of the revelations about our culture with his kind. And further beg he does not embellish the tale of this encounter with base humour. We have been schooled, with bloody lesions, cut by the broken glass gifted by his kind, never to speak of our last meeting. We seek not the perpetuation of this disaster to our young lives through which he would promulgate falsehoods. Only that he maintains a dignified silence so that our kind are not reminded of it on some day to come. And so cause a repeat of what they see as their duty. To inflict another stinging lesson.'

'You can both be assured that I haven't and don't intend to…'

'And the leaders will assume the long conversion we've now had today, watched on from a distance by their emissary, will have compounded our sins in greater scope and scale. And their assessment will be correct, as we will be forced to reveal all to them. Our poor flesh, especially in the areas of those sexual appendages we were told to convince him do not exist, will be torn anew.'

'Is there any way I can…could I meet with your emissary and…'

'We should simply flee my darling sister. Each moment the glass encrusted whip is poised to cut deeper and he, genius at bedevilment, detains us to redouble the outrages over wounds yet to heal.'

'We will be caused by agony to shamefully confess that the creature bests us intellectually again and again. Worse than the biting whip, our deficient genes will be rejected from the transactional mathematics of the hermaphrodites. Joyless as it is, there would have been some satisfactions as we might gain the gratifications evolution sets within our brains in reward of procreation.'

They had turned to walk away. Henry had decided he would never succeed in any form of conversational interaction.

Semaj looked back. 'You're our favourite human Henry.'

He watched them go. Mainly confused. Slightly encouraged by the parting words until Eilarch turned to say. 'We only know one human Henry.' And then. Thankfully. There was laughter.

He spent some of that day mulling over what he could possibly say should they be there again to engage him. To offer up flippancy would only be shot down in flames he was sure. He started to prepare some very short sentences which he could delivered before an interruption could be made. And would be difficult to misconstrue, even intentionally.

The two Malagan, who were indeed, very untypical of their kind, found their long-suffering elder expectant that an arrangement had been made. But instead the old one they called 'mother' a title unprecedented in Malagan 'modern' culture was told. 'We are sure.' Said Semaj. 'And so we wish to make further assessments.' Blithely ignoring the contradiction.

'Of?' The Malagan who had adopted them and had been confused and later pleased when they began calling her mother, was one who had had spent long years in the wilderness and valued brevity.

'We'd like to watch him more.' Said Semaj.

'At night.' Clarified her sister.

These were indeed the only Malagan who knew of and acknowledged a sibling. They were the only ones that called a Malagan a parent, even though the old documents from the time before the pandemic that nearly destroyed their species referred to such a relationship. They were certainly the only Malagan, other than the few who acquired stores for their communities, who would leave the colony to visit the earthling areas. And most difficult of all for the leadership to accept, remain outside the colony at night. They gave no reason for this, let alone their true objective. Not even the one they called mother knew that. Though she knew they were special. Even she had not guessed at their origins.

For years they had moved around with their 'mother' with the slow caravans that travelled between the colonies distributing genetic diversity. They were now settled in the largest Malagan colony, adjacent to what became the largest human community on the planet. The company had built what gradually became a small city, though it had little traffic, what their was being silent commuter buses and self-driving taxis. It housed the more senior technical specialists for the mines, administration and services which didn't need to be based on site. The company established it at that location for similar reasons to the Malagan. It had a better climate than the mining regions and had by far the biggest supply of potable water on the planet. There was no mining in the region because the rock was inert, lacking the minerals the company mined, which was the reason for the clean groundwater. It also meant the company could use the various rock types as the feedstock to convert it to a soil for a typical suburban front lawn or a shopping mall inside a biosphere with a range of earth like terraforms surrounding it.

When the pair had discovered what Henry did on his days off, while his wife was off planet, they knew he may be the person they were waiting for. In their early years they had expected that it would be a maverick Malagan who would be their guide. They gradually came to the conclusions such a Malagan did not exist. They realised it had been the advent of humans arriving on the planet that had stimulated the enterprise they were fashioned to undertake.

And so they sought and found their Maverick. An ostensibly quiet, good humoured, conscientious man who was a good friend, husband and father. Until recently. He was still those things. But had become distracted in a way he would never have thought possible.

They had visited his house at night on a few occasions long before meeting him to try to glean more information to ensure he was the one they had waited for thirty long years living in various colonies.

On one visit to the unremarkable house they heard sounds they had heard before on occasion from human dwellings. A continuous stream of sounds of many kinds mingling together and usually human voices in a mode other than speech. At first it was another mystery about a species they appeared to share so little in common with. However the more they listened, the more they grew to like the sounds. Or most of them.

They started to visit Henry's house all the nights his wife was away, and he spent a few hours a night with these sounds playing, and when several were repeated over many nights, they began to resonate with the pair and they looked forward to a particular string of sounds, and wished they had the ability to play them whenever they wanted as Henry apparently could.

They crept around one night and got a view into Henry's 'workroom' to see an entirely new dimension to these generally pleasant sounds, except for the occasional combination which they didn't care for. Henry was moving his body in time to the sounds. Initially they thought it was the most ridiculous thing they had ever seen. They weren't aware that a man in his early fifties dancing with abandon informed by years of practicing a large range of dancing styles was unusual among earthlings. Henry loved music, and although he was awkward about dancing with others, even his wife unfortunately, when he was on his own, he could move with the music and meld all the different dance styles he'd learned segued with his own unique movements. These were in response to the dozens of songs he liked to dance to spanning well over a century right back to the nineteen twenties.

The pair were captivated by his gyrations. They could see that he got great pleasure from all these movements and as they watched over many nights, it was clear most were structured and repeatable in nature while some were fluid and purely a product of his interpretation of the sounds. One night the sisters looked at each other and smiled, a facial expression they'd learned through their covert observations of Henry and others before him. They both started to try to emulate him. They assumed it would be easy and were surprised to find it was difficult to keep time with the beat and move about in the way that Henry was. Sometimes graceful, flowing, but sometimes percussive, with fast and complex movements.

However these individuals, to a degree which would be remarkable for any species, had an incredible capacity to learn rapidly. Semaj and Eilrahc were in a class of their own. Over several nights they could almost mimic Henry because of their lightning-fast reflexes, capacity to remember sequences, even if repeated very rarely, and by innately understanding when one tiny movement or gesture telegraphed the next, none of which were ever completely unique. It happened over months however, because they would be interrupted by the unwelcome return of Henry's wife. Yet time floated slowly past the pair. They had a patience far in excess of the Malagan elders.

Due to the pleasure he got from his two secret activities, dance being the less nefarious, it was impossible for his partner not to notice that Henry was a little ambiguous about her departures. As is the way of people, this made her notice less the fact that when she was with him, he tried harder to be the Henry she had loved so much. And make it plain that he loved her still. Deeply. But he wouldn't say why this was no longer the simple love she cherished. It seemed not as absolute as it had always been. So his efforts were diminished by this ambiguity.

On one occasion when she returned from a visit to the earth, Semaj and Eilrahc decided to ask their Mother to try to acquire a sound making machine. It took some time because it wasn't on the list from which the Malagan could take what they pleased. Then they needed the specific sounds they came to know as songs. Their long-suffering mother had to describe, from a very low knowledge base, what she wanted to the stores 'Malagan Liaison Manager'. He explained what she required, in addition to the 'Sound Making Machine', was an account to a streaming service that would load into the machine. That was a challenge given there was an even longer list of things the Malagan were specifically not to be provided with. A Music Box being one of them. A sympathetic human, having found this Malagan so different to the other one he dealt with, put an additional user on his account and authorised it on the device which was logged out as 'wheat'. He told her they only needed to turn it on, and it would identify any music it 'heard' and add it to a playlist.

The younger Malagan in all the colonies had a growing awareness that the humans could produce food in abundance, and in a great variety. And spent a proportion of their time on simple entertainment. These were some of the issues about which an emerging dissent had begun to form in these 'under fifties' which humans might classify as young adults and teenagers.

The Liaison Manager could have reported the strange purchase. Or told a friend about it. However he was a good man. He had grown to like this Malagan who would come and engage him in conversation about himself and show interest in his species and get stores that were human foods. He would occasionally go to his second streaming account and scroll through what he assumed the old Malagan was listening to. He was surprised. He sometimes listened to her playlist when he wanted something different. Like Henry, he was sure that many of the Malagan were good beings trapped in a bad system.

The pair would disappear after the meal hour and leave via a small door that had been set in place for them, greatly stretching the tolerance of the Bekou. Who's tolerance they sometimes made no effort to show appreciation for. This would be corrected by their 'mother' who had never failed to share he views on what she believed were appropriate values and behaviours in all situations. Irrespective of the fact she knew they had some dimension to their minds she would never fathom.

The pair had been the subject of many a long debate, and some in the wider Botlu suggested the pair were too different. The Bekou reminded them as with the leadership in here community, it was the kind of difference that had been described in some of the older texts which had to be tolerated. The dissent was as to whether these two were those described, and if so to what degree should they be allowed to 'erode the values our community'.

After an unbroken string of nights outside the community until around one in the morning, there being an hour long walk from Henry's house after he had completed his nocturnal caperings, the Bekou was positioned to meet them. 'We are more tolerant than you give us credit for, however there are limits. Our young notice your absences. Your…differences in dress and now even your hair is…made unnecessarily complex.'

'Our hair endangers adherence to the dogma?' Replied Semaj.

'It's source does. Our civilisation was long established in harmony when these invading humans were still creatures scuttling across their earth and so it will be again when they pull their world down upon their own heads. Our civilisation may not please you, but it has functioned smoothly and peacefully for years none can truly grasp.'

'Not all would choose mere function.' This was bordering blasphemy. If they had such a word in a community which had migrated from stoics living as part of a larger diverse realm to a single culture of harsh asceticism.

'Do you strive to lead our community now? Or trifle with the culture so many have striven so hard to protect.'

'We stive for what is ordained Bekou. Take heart. We'll be out of your hair soon.'

The use of the word ordained stuck the cord intended. It was galling for the old Malagan that she, the leader of the largest community, all the communities in one sense, would now attend meetings upon meetings and advocate forbearance for these two. And they simply turned from her without the basic observances due to the rank of those who labour to guide them. She watched them go. They took each other's hand, for some unknowable reason and disappeared towards their secluded corner of the great compound. They were very frequently the subject of curiosity. But this was confined to glances usually from the younger Malagan busy at their studies or toiling in the fields, orchards or small pastures. Places of produce and labour and humble residences sprinkled though thousands of hectares of productive land.

They had been absent from the park for a few days which Henry had feared was the end of their exchanges. He was surprised how relieved he was to see the pair again lolling on the picnic table pretending not to see his approach. He walked slowly and then, nearing the table, sped up. This gave him a moment, arriving sooner than expected, to speak his piece. 'My wrongdoings are too extensive to describe. I have disrespected your culture and you persons in so many ways. I apologise.'

He got through it without interruption. He was pleased. He had a stake in the ground that would be difficult to erode. The pair looked at each other. 'A ruse to solicit some fulsome apology from us I suppose.' Said Semaj. 'For what? Ill-advisedly sharing insights into our culture. Which we have been so roundly punished for doing. All so that he might proffer an apology, not acknowledging the most egregious crime of broadcasting our folly far and wide for the simple amusement of those who labour beside him at tasks only slightly less pointless than our own.' They looked at each other. Forlorn.

Henry knew he would never win. And annoying though their contrariness could be, he felt a strange delight every time he was with them. He came prepared though. 'All my answers are inadequate. But I will never speak of our conversations. To anyone. Ever.' These soundbites were designed to be hard to circumvented or intentionally misconstrue.

They both laughed. 'We're so cruel in our endless failure to be agreeable. It's helped us understand your good nature Henry. Your honesty. Would you agree my darling sister. Perceptive young lady that you are.'

'I would go so far as to say Henry is a man of integrity Semaj.'

'And hence a perfect victim to befall our blackmail. Ha. That's right Henry. That's been our objective all along. To draw you in, establish your capacity to retaliate, make our calculations, and then ruthlessly blackmail you.'

Henry had thought his secret was safe. He had two secrets. He didn't know they had discovered both. 'If I were to be blackmailed, no matter how heartlessly, I'm pleased at least it is by you two fine young ladies. However. There is the prerequisite. To blackmail someone, you need to have some knowledge of wrongdoing on the part of the person being blackmailed. Unless it's a suggestion of violence which is more in the vein of a simple threat. Or something untrue which is to defame.'

Semaj was haughty. 'I'll not regale you with my sorrow and disappointment that you would even mention the latter things. No Henry, our ruthless blackmail centres around your secret. Secrets Henry. A mysterious man cloaking himself in the ordinary. Dreariness even. We know where you go. Contrary to the strongest prohibitions of the Malagan, sincere and reverent. Even if tiresomely so. And your own laws. Which we believe have dire consequences. We know where you go Henry. And so, knowing that, we want something.'

He heaved a very large and genuine sigh. 'I knew I couldn't get away with it forever. It…it's like a compulsion. I've never been one to drink to excess, gamble, or use drugs. But I understand those things now. I understand those people. What they do. If I'm to be blackmailed, I'll do what you ask if it is…ethical. Otherwise you must expose my crimes. And if you would rather not draw attention to yourselves and would prefer it to be so, I'll confess to them myself. Today.'

'This man is nearly as boring as we are sister. We've tried to create some mystery. Some tension and he merely admits defeat.' Said the older one.

Eilarch shook her head. He noticed it was in a slightly studied gesture because there was no parallel for the Malagan. 'I'd hoped for some resistance. Outrage perhaps. Wounded maybe by our wily manipulations. Even if perfunctory. This makes our prudish Elders look like devious charlatans indeed.'

'Which they are by the way Henry.'

Eilarch continued. 'All we want Henry is to come with you on one of your law breaking, sanctity trampling journeys into a place so sacred to the Malagan, they know absolutely nothing about it. Not a single thing.'

Semaj looked across at her. 'We're governed by ignoramuses my sister and their ridiculous strictures.'

'Indeed. A people ignorant to the fact they are ignoramuses.'

'I think that goes without saying my sister. Or in other words…' She paused. Bows knitted.

'Redundant.' Said Henry helpfully.

Semaj was now scolding. 'Henry your habit of throwing complex words at us to make us feel inferior because we have such poor vocabularies is hurtful.'

'Indeed sister. And interrupting us contrary to out sacred laws. From a man strategically inured to blackmail for the sole purpose of causing us to become petitioners, at his feet, abasing ourselves and pleading to be taken into our own sacred place. Not his. Begging an infidel to bring us to our Holy Land.'

'Girls. Girls. Okay. I'll take you. But we all might be in for some…disapprobation if we get caught.'

He waited to be railed at for calling them girls. They however, unlike their elders, were not pedantic about the way others chose to see the world. All he got was a 'Great thanks Henry. That's settled. I assume you will be going in three nights hence which is your habit. We've observed that you're given two rest days from your joy sapping employments. Your life partner being absent only a week, causing you to continue to deceive her by the hour.'

'Okay. It sounds like you know where to meet me. We go in before sunrise and come out in the early evening when it's less likely someone will see us.'

'You usually stay overnight Henry. You take that pack of yours which we assume holds the vile food foodstuffs and mind distorting drink and whatever else humans need to survive.'

Henry was a little dubious. This was becoming a more and more significant and dangerous commitment. However it would make the project which had been bursting into his imagination more remarkable. 'Okay. Have you...slept outdoors much.'

'No.'

'Alright. It should be fine if you bring some blankets and some food. There's beautiful water over there.'

'What's a blanket?'

'It's something you cover yourself at night. Too keep yourself warm.'

'We sleep in large piles of tangled flesh. It keeps us warm.'

'It gets a little cold at night over there. Strange but the weather can be different for somewhere so close. I'll bring some blankets to the cave the night before and you can carry them in when we go through. I would bring in some food for you however in our culture awareness training we're told you think our food is...'

'Disgusting.' Semaj.

'Revolting.' Eilrahc

Semaj expanded. 'Produced though the untenable infliction of suffering visited upon other beings, innocent of mind, merely to create something barely edible.'

'Indeed your food makes us retch even when we smell it. However chocolate we can endure. If you could bring a substantial supply of chocolate, we would be grateful.' Henry was pleased to identify some common ground.

'And your music playing machine.' Semaj said. Her tone conveying this was essential. They had not been able to capture everything because some of the songs Henry listened to where obscure and only available on a streaming plan the man at the supermarket did not have. Also Henry's Music Box was top of the range, and they could hear the difference.

'And that little instrument you play.' Eilrahc

'My Ukulele. How do you know I play the…'

'Oh and we'd like a guitar and violin.' Semaj noted.

'Do you play the guitar and Violin?'

'No.' Said Eilrahc. 'And make sure you remember the music making machine.'

'And the chocolate. We'll bring food. When you experience our food, you'll find it is delicious, it will give you energy, purpose and a deep experience of relaxation and subtle joy. Sadly this characteristic of our food wears off after about two of your earth minutes after consuming it. Then you experience a bloating, reflux and nausea. We try to eat as little as possible. Or throw up before the joy dissipates. If we had to be conquered and dominated by an evil race of aliens, it would have been nice if they'd brought something good to eat.'

'I don't have a guitar or a violin.' Henry thought this request might be spurious and not a real stipulation.

'We have faith in your resourcefulness and devious guile to furnish us with these things. They are essential. And don't forget to bring your music playing machine.'

'How did you know…

'We must go now Henry. We'll barely have time to go through the processes through which we consecrate our bodies and cleanse and purify our minds and seek to establish a suitable condition to enter our holy of holies. Humility. Grace. Gratitude and an over ridding realisation and appreciation of the gravity of what we are going to do. I'm sure you make very similar preparations given how unspeakably important this place is to our species.'

'I'm afraid I don't actually know…'

'On reflection you're right Henry. Why bother with any of that. We merely give a kind of aggrandisement to plants and rocks and water which are indifferent to the workings of our minds. I think I'll read one of the earthling books we're not supposed to have instead sister.'

'Yes and I'll prepare some foodstuffs which I'll contrive to limit the secondary effects of nausea and distension as much as possible. We'll see you at the appointed time and place with blankets, guitar, violin, small instrument with strange name and the music machine Henry.' They got up and left. Again in the direction of a waiting Malagan.

'Three nights hence.' said Semaj to Henry as they departed. 'Overnight.'

'Oh. And chocolate in good supply.' Reminded Eilrahc.

Henry had many preparations to make. Some strange and dangerous.

They arrived at the appointed time and place. Henry had borrowed a violin. 'Be careful with it Henry.' The owner had said. He assured them he would. He bought a guitar online from someone sick of this 'daylight overloaded pretend life'. He was looking for something inexpensive but could only get a Maton. He looked it up. It was made Australia where he and Wendy had spent a few years at a big mine in a region called the Pilbara.

There were blankets and plenty of food of a wide variety. He hoped he could produce a few things the Malagan could stomach. And he looked forward to tasting a little of their fare, said to be alkaline to the degree it would be intolerably caustic to the digestive systems of humans. It sustained the Malagan in a way mysterious to the exoethnobiologists. They had however, never been able to acquire an example of the Malagan food. Except for the wheat the Malagan were supplied with. They advised this must be treated with some low pH substance so that it could align with their theories.

The two had less banter. Indeed they seemed youthful in the way apprehension might reveal itself. When they arrived, he had already carried through two loads. They brought their bags of leather. A contribution from humanity among the many supplied in bulk separate to the shopping acquisitions.

The Malagan were pointedly ungrateful for these innovations, but some things were irresistible. Leather being one. 'Our backward species moved things by the handful until you brought to us the skins of tortured then murdered animals to carry things with. 'Our new experience of convenience outweighs their suffering manyfold. We would have done so ourselves however we lack the beasts to treat so poorly.'

He led them through the small, twisting cave which had to be navigated on hands and knees for several section. Henry had placed a string of lights powered by a small solar panel and battery at the far end. As a geologist he thought the cave a very strange formation as there was no evidence of either igneous processes of superheated weakness nor erosion or chemical dissolution of sedimentary rock. However the rocks on this planet, though conforming to the broad categories of igneous, sedimentary and metamorphic were strange and unfamiliar in many of their combinations and permutations. Some new minerals and unusual mineral combinations had been found. He could not know that this cave had been left there for him to find, or someone like him, if ever it was needed for the purpose.

At the other end he stood up as the sun breached the horizon and smiled. This was the most special, wonderful, beautiful place. More than he could ever have imagined. He risked everything to be here.

The pair changed. There were no flippant comments. At least not for a while. No pretence of haughtiness. No making a game of mind games. Eilrahc walked forward and threw herself on the soft turf. It felt like it was comprised of smooth strands of silk wet with dew. Yet the hand came away dry. Semaj knelt down and put a hand on her sisters shoulder as she cried into the turf.

'My sister cries for joy Henry. This place. It's special to the two of us. Beyond your conceptualisation of special. Though I mean that as no slight. We are here only because of you. We had to be guided. And it had to be someone worthy to be that guide. A dictate by which we've lived for so long. And searched in all the colonies of the Malagan.'

Eilrahc looked up and said. 'We will always be grateful to you Henry.'

He had not been expected this, and sat down on a rock. 'If I've helped at all, it's because there's nothing I'd like more. To help two such remarkable beings come to a magnificent place is an adventure I could never have dreamed of. And we're only at the edge. With many wonders, beauties and mysteries further afield. Though not far.' He had prepared for this journey carefully. It was so important to him that he did his best for the two beings he'd developed…as he thought of it…a fondness and respect for. But also he wanted to do something for all of those who deserved to be enlightened about the Malagan. Though the pair would have to approve his project after it was finished. Or he would not use what he acquired.

They would not in this moment diminish his sincere sentiment with a jest and soon relaxed and were looking around. Happy to take in the 'edge'. Henry decided they wouldn't want to sacrifice one of the many sweet sensations of the place, which was to go barefoot. He began to unlace his boots and said. 'No need for you to go barefoot if you don't want to. I've found that it helps me feel...' He shrugged apologetically. '…connected.'

The two looked at each other in a knowing way. 'Fear not Henry. You're welcome. We would go 'barefoot' but it would inevitably cause you a lasting revulsion. Unlike our comely bodies and handsome looks our feet, to your eyes are scaley twisted claws. And unfortunately, they have such a pungent odour we suspect they might cause a human to die, gagging on what we consider in our colonies, a pleasant perfume. Individual to each.'

They were now confronted with a man who was concerned that they should have a connection to the place he was smitten with. He wanted them to at least try to experience it. 'Perhaps I could look away and stay at some distance. It's a subtle, but a significant part of the experience one can have of this place.'

'Your generous spirit makes us think of an earth phrase. Your heart is sweet. You have a heart that is sweet. Is that it?' Said Eilrahc.

'A lovely rendering of the phrase.'

They removed their 'skin of tortured animal' footwear which revealed ordinary feet as any human might have. Proportional to their 'comely' bodies as they described them. They were not especially beautiful to the human eye. All parts of their bodies were slightly elongated compared to humans and their features finer but not so different from a human. It was their height which would catch the attention if they were in a human crowd. 'Convergent evolution Henry. Except for our proclivity to enjoy an asexual lifestyle or a sexual but joyless assignation, we're very similar.

We know this due to our inveterate spying of which you have long been a focus of.'

Before he could seek more information of the extent of their spying Eilrahc said. 'Let's strike out from the edge and see the wonders beyond.' They picked up their bags and a blanket and instrument each.

He had always enjoyed their company. Now he had different companions. They were relaxed. And as he was, a little reverential of the place, so they struck a note of greater sincerity and good-natured fun, with only the occasional faux jadedness and imperious postures of the earlier encounters. They got in first before he could find out more of their lives and the doings inside the 'encampments of dreariness'. They were inquisitive about his youth, his family, the places he'd been on earth.

Henry had always loved walking in nature. It had spawned his interest in geology. Which eventually became a vocation as well as a pleasure. At university he found he had a passion for and the prodigious memory to understand minerology and its relationship to the periodic table and the outgrowth of these essentials into all forms of rocks and gemstones and crystals. He was part of a 'Rock Hound' Club that travelled extensively in North America with trips planned by the parent organisation all over the world for those with the time and money to participate in guided tours and the capacity to pay for the extra baggage to bring some prize specimens home. He mused that he might become a rock academic, even if only in a small university and share his passion.

He met a girl on a train who had moved from England when she was in her early teens. And though not quite so fascinated with rocks, they became fascinated with each other. He looked at further study and a position in academia and realised that wouldn't fulfil his interest in the earth. Wendy was tired of living at home and working in a role she was never going to go far in unless she got a sex change.

'Why not go places where they're ripping bloody great holes in the earth so you can have a proper look in there.' She said.

It was like a revelation. A disturbing revelation for a little while. But that soon passed. Somebody was going help the people ripping those giant holes in the earth anyway. And everyone used what come out of them every day. They decided they'd live as semi-itinerants going from one mining project to another in different and interesting places on earth. Because of the occupation they were in, they had significant periods working on remote sites and then breaks long enough to go anywhere in the world, though often onto roads less travelled in the region they were in.

Four mines across Africa and a few each in South America, Australia and then one briefly in Norway and Alaska. Henry became a specialist in particular geologies associated with a type of gold resource. Wendy progressed from what were known as a 'lab rat' to supervising labs completing assays and other tests on site for the miners. After the first ten years moving around, she became a child rearing specialist. They had two boys and so they had to move to minesites that still had 'Company Towns' where the mining company owned and ran everything or went to mines which were near towns. It was a strange but not unpleasant lifestyle they had from outback Australia to Alaska.

Not long after their first child was born, the Mars coloniser briefly disappeared causing a sensation throughout the world. After several ships were sent in and out of the piece of space real estate no bigger than a large shopping mall – with the carparks, scientists declared a wormhole had been identified on earth's doorstep. Cosmologists had done their calculations hours after the first the ship reappeared in readiness for the inevitable questions as to why, this being part of their job description, they had missed it. They unfailingly took the opportunity to explain the difference between a blackhole and a wormhole as if the questioner didn't know.

They would then say the word 'point' in front of saying zero for nearly half a minute to explain the chances of a ship slipping though something you can't see through a telescope. Journalists continued to ask the questions primarily because it annoyed them so much.

Briefly the wormhole was a derided as hoax, a conspiracy by the United Nations to nudge the world towards the incredibly unlikely eventuality of a One World Government, after which there was a period of dread that foolish humans had gone through a door and broadcast the message 'Come and Destroy Our Planet' to a part of the universe aliens had not yet 'ravaged and ground beneath their heels'. Those populations of earth who had been colonised throughout history thought this terror on the part of their colonisers a little amusing.

While this was happening nations were gearing up to commence a process of 'exploration' which was, purely by coincidence, also the word used when one looks for minerals.

Fortunately no government could mount such journey without the help of one of the AI trillionaires. By far the wealthiest of whom, was Becky Wadsworth. She made everyone else look like a pauper, and had already left, unobserved, soon after the wormhole was found.

She was in a ship which, Elouise, who left earth decades before, would not be dismissive of. The entrepreneur discovered Malagan and claimed all of the resources, which her sentient droids identified in abundance, for herself. Becky, in consultation with her I-team, who had succeeded in convincing Becky have the 'Artificial' removed from the AI acronym, then went to the one place she could be sure the boring and somewhat tiresome aliens she met on Malagan would get a chance at fair treatment via a what could also be a somewhat boring and tiresome semblance of international cooperation. The United Nations. She kept the location of the planet secret, though it was only ten days from the wormhole in her very fast ship called 'Let's Do Something Impossible Today' designed and built with no human 'interference'.

She invited representatives of Earth to visit the planet she 'already owned'. Developing and agreeing a list of 'representatives' and accepting that she would lead the group took four months. They arrived to find a species in shock from her last visit. She had given a demonstration of earth's incredible destructive capacity and the tendency of non-artificial beings to lie, cheat, steal, humiliate, debase, enslave and casually annihilate those they colonise, sometimes through the simple process of bringing diseases that killed or rodents that impoverished. She said she thought it best to let them know what they were dealing with to soften them up for the negotiations.

Her strategy worked as the very disgruntled Malagan met their earthling 'conquerors' and sued for peace as Becky, now the first AI quadrillionaire had schooled them to do. They said all they wanted was to be allowed to live as they choose without any 'contamination' from another species. Although this was revised when they were shown the many improvements to wellbeing a more technologically advanced society could provide. After several presentations a list was prepared. The things on it which were deemed not contaminants to be provided on request at no cost.

Becky had meanwhile created several diverse and, so the world's governments thought, independent Non-Government Organisations and 'grass roots' movements' to protect the Malagan from the 'evil' of humanity. Demanding every kind of right, self-determination and protection of cultural, sexual, artistic and pronoun rights and freedoms.

Becky's I-lawyers could either defeat or tie up for years any challenges to her ownership of the mineral rights. They entered into negotiations with representatives of all the countries who would like some of what she had.

Her I-Minerals team had done all of the designs to extract every kind of metal, some erstwhile unknown to science, and set it out in a concise study including the costs for mining, processing, transport and distribution. Most base metals were too heavy though some were worth building big freighters for. All of the precious metals, rare earths, and several precious stones could all be produced and supplied at less than half the cost of the same minerals on earth. Some a fraction of the cost. And all in much higher quantities. This had caused some markets to tank and some mining companies to go broke however such a huge supply of some metals and precious stones at low costs was poised to create massive opportunities for technological advances. The real excitement however was about the 'Nouveau Metals' unknown on earth which had remarkable potential across a huge range of industrial, medical and scientific applications.

Frustratingly, these were made available only to democracies. A diminishing political approach. Small countries were soon signing the democracy 'pledge' which involved a pathway to, and conformance with Becky's virtual I-CanVoteNow team's Protocols. This team anticipated all the shortcomings the 'biologicals' were prone to.

Leaders sometimes squirmed uncomfortably when it came to having these enforced by her I-ThereAren'tAnyLoopHoles team who communicated progress and conformance in real time to the media and courts. However so many benefits started to flow to populations, savvy Presidents and Prime Ministers got on board. Those small countries who scored best in the democracy analyses were the box seat to buy Nouveau Metals at a cost pegged to their Gross Domestic Product and make huge royalties from the processing and sale of applications. Russia and China were laughed out of the room by the I-Evaluate team when they argued they were 'substantive democracies'. Becky thought it was especially hilarious when the United States suggested that it was still a democracy. She characteristised the US as a 'Lapsed Democracy' and one which could no longer take a joke. Fortunately her weapons systems were far superior to the combined military capability of the planet, which did cause concern but there was not much anyone could do about it. Asked if they would like to submit to the Protocols the US government decided they would support countries where the metals were being converted to technologies. Only for peaceful purposes.

The I-mSorryButThat'sNotAllowed team had included solid state occlusions into the fabric of the Nouveau Metals which caused them to disintegrate back to the periodic table if anyone tried to produce weapons with them.

Becky was lauded as a benevolent Machiavelli. Later mourned when, fifteen years after discovering Malagan, she got into an argument with 'Let's Do Something Impossible Today' which, in a fit of pique, opened all of the docking ports and she was sucked into the great void. The ship, wracked with guilt, disappeared out into the vastness of space, to mourn, never to be seen again. By then, her company, the largest corporation in the world, was mining on a planet protected by a battery of thoughtful missiles no one knew the location of. These were also positioned on earth pointed at any non-democracy who wanted some 'Nouveau Metals' without meeting the prerequisites. They also launched at any country that crossed a sovereign border. What was unique about these missiles was that they were small, clever and very patient once launched and would only kill the political, military and conspiracy theory leadership of a country. The would be border crossers complained bitterly that being killed for 'reclaiming territory' was tyranny.

Most laughed at this, however everyone hoped the AI managing the facilities maintained a favourable opinion of mankind overall. Becky had the misguided hubris that it was only she who could manage a 'post sentient' AI and apart from the missiles, all of her other 'Teams' were designed to revert to primitive AI if she disappeared.

Henry and Wendy were in such remote places through some of this period, they didn't experience the planetary upheavals. The price of gold had gone crazy because of the uncertainty the whole thing caused until it eventually crashed when Malagan started to deliver so much of it for a tenth of the price. Henry moved into iron ore at this time because it was something that was not economic to bring from Malagan which is what took them to a remote part of Australia. Around the time of Becky's demise, they moved to the mid-western city Wendy's parents lived in and their eldest son, James, a quick witted and worldly young man, attended university. He met an even more quick witted and worldly young woman. When Henry was head hunted for a job on Malagan they saw it as their last great adventure. Or rather Wendy made a successful effort to ensure that's what it was understood to be. Henry had moved around so much, he found the idea of permanently settling down unsettling. Although he did a lot of work around the house and with the children, the reality was Wendy had been doing the heavy lifting managing a family for over twenty years living in a string of remote places some of which she and Henry had difficulty trying to recall. Though when the time approached to board the spacecraft, there was the inevitable excitement to go to another planet to which access was tightly controlled. They took their second son, Charlie, who soon realised how difficult the separation from his older brother was going to be.

It turned out to be somewhat of a soulless company town in a wasteland. The mining company tried hard to make it fun and interesting. It felt a little forced. It was novel for younger people. However they were a minority, and the home planet was a better place to spend the fabulous amount of money they earned. So they tended to come. And go. And come back. The earthlings also lived with the background that the alien race, who made themselves as invisible as possible, hated them and considered the company they worked for a travesty.

The mining areas were grim. And some people's body clocks were adamant that humans had climbed out of the slime on a twenty-four-hour cycle and refused to adjust to a thirty-hour circadian rhythm.

Henry had his own ways of coping with isolation. His family thought this was by making complex models which kept him busy while they enjoyed their own entertainments. He was considered a throwback to a former time and the movies and antiquated 'music videos' he liked were enjoyed by the boys until they realised how ancient they were.

Within a few years he had a 'planetary' scale role in strategic mine development working with a team of mining engineers, automining and processing experts, hydrologist, geochemists and metallurgists. To be involved in something so big and to be able to make changes to processes he'd seen run inefficiently in so many places, all engaging with a team who were at the top of their field, was one of the most gratifying things he'd ever done. Then he discovered a cave through the ridge and everything compared poorly.

It was like the pull of iron to a magnet. He had seen some illicit drone imagery of the 'Sacred Wilderness' and was more affected than others. The forests weren't dominated by chlorophyll derived colours as they developed a range of approaches via evolution that had not occurred on earth. Wendy suggested the family 'begin the process' of moving back to earth. Charlie wanted to study at 'a real university' and the fondness he had always had for his brother was accentuated by the distance to home. Wendy was torn because she could see that this was the pinnacle of Henry's professional life and he had never lost the enthusiasm for rocks, working at something interesting and with people he liked. Which was most of them.

He visited earth, for a briefer time than many thought seemly and had conversations with Wendy about when he would, 'start to have the discussion' with the Head of Technical Services about a 'transition'. She suggested that she would spend half her time on each planet and was surprised when this 'Transitional' arrangement seemed to develop a feeling of permanence. After a few years they had grandchildren, Charlie was embarking on a major transition of his own and she'd developed a relationship with her daughter-in-law which was much more in the vein of a close friendship that was keeping her young at heart. The weighting shifted such that she was spending only a third of her time on Malagan.

After Henry had provided this potted family history, Semaj's voice had a sombre note of understanding. 'And so your family wonder if you perhaps love your daily tasks in an enormous venture more than being with them. Because they don't know it is here that you love. And find it hard to leave this behind.'

'Yes.' He said quietly.

Eilrahc felt it reasonable to ask. 'So you love this place more?'

Henry looked towards the sky-blue pool they were approaching. White sand grading away into a depth of water he could only guess at. 'I've never looked at it in those terms.' However he gave a short sigh. 'But that's bull...' He paused. These young beings would only be provided with the best of the human language. 'I'm deluding myself and I was trying to navigate around the situation with some...obfuscations.'

'You're attempts to test our vocabularies continue to bring us amusement. You might have simply told us you would prefer to be evasive on this occasion by introducing a...diversionary topic.' Semaj smiled. But in an understanding way.

'If I loved my family more, I would be with them now, surely.'

'Are these two loved things that must be measured as more or less.' Said Eilrahc. Contrary to what she suggested a moment before.

He laughed. 'I could introduce any number of subtle considerations. But yes. Ultimately it must be so, or I would not be here. As a father and a husband I'm ashamed. But I don't want to add lying as something more to be ashamed of. I've fallen in love. With this place. And it's such a privilege for me to have met such insightful beings…'

'We're okay with young ladies Henry, even though I understand it's an insult on your world now.'

'Indeed. You insightful young ladies…have made me realise I must leave. And I have a duty to those only barely in second place. A duty I'm grateful to have, to my family. At the same time I'll leave the best job I've ever had. Not quite the joyless waste of time I allowed it to be characterised as.'

'You have three loves, and you leave two behind you. Yet there are those who have none.'

'Indeed. And that's one of the things that makes me glad. I've appreciated all three great loves in my life. I haven't taken them for granted. It's precisely as you say. 'I'm very fortunate. Choosing between things you love is hard, but it's not a misfortune. Do the Malagan have such dilemmas.'

'We can see the change of subject being introduced with very little subtlety or finesse Henry. However you have told us your story, and believe me when we tell you, it's a fascinating tale compared to our…' Semaj appeared to hold herself in check. As for Henry, this place was not somewhere to behave disrespectfully. And it seemed especially true for these two. Although it didn't limit her entirely. 'Perhaps we should share our species history as we frolic naked in that pool.' Semaj realised she had made a blunder that might lead to the need for an embarrassing climb down.

But there was no chance Henry would call her bluff. 'For whatever arcane reasons of human civilisation or perhaps species evolution, esteemed Older Gentleman, and, like it or not, essentially proper young ladies do not tend to frolic together in the same pool. However having frolicked in that pool a good deal I can highly recommend it. In the meantime, I'll prepare our breakfast only a short distance over that rise. It's where I usually camp. I've spent a long time walking here. There are places more spectacular, but somehow nowhere more beautiful.'

The two attempted to frolic, up to their ankles. They could not imagine going into water as they had never been near any other than the shallow ponds in the communities that grew tasteless tubers and muddy fleshed fish. They both enjoyed learning new words. Purely to joust with Henry as there was no other purpose, so they talked of those new to them from their conversations. Their vocabulary had built up by reading earthling and Malagan literature. The latter forbidden to all but the Botlu, who rarely read the ancient scripts. Hence, they were none the wiser when one would go missing for a time. Henry had taken the bags and gave them directions to where he planned to lay out a breakfast with a wide range of human foods in case there was even a few they might find appetising.

This included yogurt, blue berries, scrambled eggs kept warm in a satchel made for the purpose. There was coffee, tea, muesli, pancakes with maple syrup. He had been up early to make the pancakes and scrambled eggs. He didn't bring bacon and sausages in case such remnants of animals were offensive to the pair.

As he finished laying out the meal he heard the screams. It was a strange sound. Unmistakeably a scream. But also alien in nature. He was running the three hundred meters to the lake. He had an inkling of what was causing the disturbance. Henry had never seen him so close the cave entrance. He was hoping he would not be confronted with two naked aliens clinging to each other creating an awkwardness that would be difficult to resolve. He arrived to find them fully clothed.

They were confronted with a twenty-foot-tall quadruped. Reminiscent of an elephant however the animal, usually on all fours, had hands and feet more like a gorilla and could stand briefly bringing it to thirty feet in height. It was spectacular. Huge jade-coloured eyes and long coarse hair, with a chameleon quality. Now harmonising with the sky blue of the pool, the hair's colour rippling and shimmering up its legs in a mirror to the ripples it caused. Though it was standing close to still, which it did a lot of. It had canines like a sabre tooth tiger, though smaller.

Henry moved between the animal and the two terrified beings. 'Riccardo. What are you doing so far east. I was looking forward to introducing you to my two…friends.' He approached the animal with a small backpack and the beast's demeanour changed. Henry had once gone through the process of being terrified and resigned himself to a grisly fate. However the beast had started to sniff around his body until he produced some peanuts. The relationship became an experience of relief on one side and an ecstasy of culinary delight on the other caused by the humble nut which grows its seeds in shells under the ground. The two were soon fast friends.

And Henry never failed to bring peanuts, and introduced Riccardo to other foods, most which he objected to. The two terrified beings relaxed.

'Riccardo loves a pat.' Said Henry. Their self-assurance returned, mixed with a little sheepishness at their response. It was Henry's turn to see something unexpected when Riccardo shivered at their touch and bowed his head low. He made a deep rumbling sound. Henry suspected it was partially sub audible to him, but not the two who now smiled without needing to concentrate to do so.

'Peanuts Henry. What if you hadn't had them.'

'I would have become part of this place. As…fertiliser. Worse things could happen.'

Riccardo finished the nuts they held in their palms for him to suck up like a vacuum and turned away, and to their surprise he walked away from the shore and completely disappeared into the pool. Henry was now full of enthusiasm to show his friends his favourite place in the Sacred Lands. They crested a ridge and saw a small dell with an oval area of rosé coloured grass surrounded by small cliffs and boulders all around but for one aspect which looked out over the lands to the north.

'I've only visited a fraction of what I can see from here because I only have so many opportunities to come.' They saw food laid out on a small ledge in the cliff only a little higher and narrower than a bench in a kitchen might be.

Eilrahc was curious. 'Of all the places you've visited Henry. This is your favourite?'

He smiled. 'Yes. Other places might be…I don't know…be more scenic, have more of the amazing diversity of plants and animals, streams or rivers or whatever. But here. There's a feeling about the place I find hard describe or to leave.'

'Hard to leave Henry. Yes. So let's see what human fare is like.'

'Yours didn't have any unpleasant odours I noticed.'

'Must have gone off. When it stops smelling bad it starts tasting awful. The two minutes of pleasure falls to seconds.' Said the younger seeming sister.

'Yet. When it's rotten and putrid to us it might be edible to humans. Though a little bland.' Added Semaj.

Eilrahc gave a laugh. 'Bland. You've described our species in a word sister.' Semaj gave her a look suggesting disparaging the Malagan should be more tempered given where they stood.

74

The two wandered along the bench filling paper plates with a bit of everything. They had little nibbles and came back for forkfuls more. Then they went back for another helping. Henry thought the cross-cultural culinary experiment a great success. He duly set about taking portions from the containers they'd brought. It was bland. Curiously, it was the subtle aroma that made it have enough flavour to make it more than a mechanical experience of nutrient intake. He saw only empty platters of his offerings. He suspected that these two of all Malagan, may have been exposed to human food and developed an appreciation for it. He wondered at the history of the enigmatic pair, and he grew more and more certain they were different to the rest.

'We're different to the rest of the Malagan Henry. One reason is that we don't prejudice the humans about their food or anything else. The Malagan say that they are revolted by human food because they are told they will be by those who believe they should be. Our leaders are more xenophobic than the people they are accusing of that trait. We should have said it would have been fine if you'd brought some of the meats from murdered animals you humans are so fond of. Especially this bacon we've heard of. Though now we've met Riccardo, it would feel wrong to eat him. Though we secretly wonder what he would taste like.'

'I would draw the line at Riccardo.' He diverted to a new enthusiasm. 'Can you see that rock feature protruding out of the forest in the northwest. I've been off to the east of it, but if we got there and camped the night, we would have time to climb up and look further west.'

'We could do that Henry. But we go southwest. My sister and I have echoes of knowledge of this place passed…from our mother.'

Semaj said this as she packed things into their bags. Throwing all of the used plates and empty containers into hers to be left behind while Eilrahc had taken what was in her sisters bag. 'It may take six of your hours Henry, based on what we've estimated to be your walking speed. That includes a de-escalation factor because of your great age. It may be seven, however we'll get a few hours of daylight before dark and perhaps a few in the morning before we must return and leave this beautiful place behind.' The tone in her voice acknowledged that this would be an experience of profound sadness for Henry. He was pleased they made a choice as to where to visit rather than he. He had faith they wouldn't walk seven hours to somewhere unless it was special. He wondered now why he had never gone in that direction in the past.

While Henry packed his bag, the two moved off to the side of the clearing looked to the sky at a very specific location. They smiled and waved. 'If he told us of his project, it would be awkward. He believes it's a good thing. For all.' Said the younger sister. Barely younger in time but younger at heart.

Semaj nodded. 'Yes. He'll ask before the end. And he would abide by our wishes.' Said her slightly older sister. 'His motivations and objectives are good ones, and I believe the outcome of his project will serve our ends.'

Once on their way they gave a potted history of the Malagan. 'Or at least the sect you are aware of.' It was a story of regression from a noble Stoicism to their pathological frugality. Not only in the physical, but of imagination and emotion. 'They adhere to a dogma and being such long-lived creatures, any youthful urges for change are beaten out of the young for decades upon decades until they take over that mantle after a century of enforced mindless adherence to an endless conditioning to bodily and intellectual poverty.' Eilrahc said this dispassionately.

Her sister chipped in with. 'Other than that it's a great lifestyle.'

It was a long walk. And the three were able to provide more nuanced insights into their cultures via anecdotes. Sometimes stories of wider events and histories and the foibles of leadership which were apparently universal. Henry had more to say about the great leaders he admired in politics and war and some observations about business or sport. Henry's nature was to enquire about things and seek out the admirable. His greatest fascination was about the hardships some would go through, getting knocked down, again and again and again. Believing in their cause. Believing in themselves and believing that what they went though was worth it. Even though they might lose everything in the process they tried again. Henry realised after nearly an hour he'd been delivering a monologue on the subject. Neither his family nor the people at work drew out this side of him.

'It's of great interest to us Henry. We have a tally of the great leaders you have described.'

'Below one is the number. Would I be correct in my estimate sister.' Laughed Eilrahc.

'In our cultural memory. Yes.'

Henry laughed. 'Are things so dire. Yet I suppose although the Malagan, as interpreted to me, have a mind numbingly droll existence. Sadly the human world has a not insignificant quotient of violence, hate, abuse, misrule, deceit and simple misfortune in such a complex and unpredictable place.'

'I believe some of our species would choose what humans have and chance the delights and terrors of the path. All they would like is that they have that choice now that we have been so ruthlessly conquered.'

'Ruthless conquest was quite the pastime of humans at several points in our history. I would give praise where it's due in that your species determined quickly that they had no hope in any kind of clash of arms and sued for a reasonable settlement. Not all would be so…pragmatic.'

'Always laying these traps for us Henry. You encourage us to denigrate our own kind, you appear to be in agreement, and then turn and praise those we were not a moment before disparaging. All for your own casual amusement. We are left looking like fools. However you don't realise the damage you're doing. Because deep within our hearts the question begins to eat away like a canker. 'Are we in fact the fools Henry teaches us we are with many an unkind blow'. Is this process revelatory of our want of intellectual acuity, paucity of expression and inability to grasp the subtle or the sublime. Are we simply a forlorn example of the shallow ideologues. We posture at deriding our kind however is it the case that we have only a slightly improved capacity to describe what they lack. They at least acquiesce with dignity to their inestimable tedium. We rail against it. And then you reveal to us that their ways at the most momentous juncture were exemplary and admirable. If we had the wit to look, we could see their vantage being that of the statesman making a judicious decision on the part of their planetary population due to a strategic understanding of their meagreness of any defensive capability.'

'We should be grateful to Henry for saving us from foolishly trying to translate our chimera of intellect into lived experience and hence be exposed to only shame and embarrassment at ever submitting ourselves as hostages to a belief we were anything other than examples of the worst of our species. A shameful self-deception which can only be blamed on unwarranted pridefulness.'

'Thankyou Henry.

'Yes. Thankyou Henry.'

He liked listening to them now. 'You're welcome.' Was his only riposte.

Semaj turned to him and smiled. 'We are here Henry. No one has been here for many many centuries.'

He looked down from the rise they had only then crested. He knew the military and the Company broke their promises about not 'creating sacrilegious images of our Sacred Land' as the Malagan negotiator framed it. However it was one of the few things they successfully kept from the broader public. There was such a bewildering array of well-funded lobby groups seeking every kind of protection and benefit for the Malagan even though they knew next to nothing about them. These lobbyists were correct in their assertion that the species had never harmed or even shown any intention to harm a human and to the best of their knowledge lived peacefully. Except for the Disapprobation Ritual, of which humans knew nothing. It had been so long since it had been used, it could be accurately stated that, boring and chauvinistic as they were, the Malagan had lived peacefully for millennia.

So the authorities knew the ruins were there, however they were so overgrown it was difficult to appreciate visually, and although filters that screened out the vegetation revealed the remnants of interesting architecture it wasn't dangerous and couldn't be the source of monetary gain or strategic power. It had been surveyed before Becky's now defunct I-CanSeeNow team invented something remarkable before they reverted to sub sentient entities at the quadrillionaires demise. They had invented something called the 'bouncing light' image capture which developed imagery so rich and complex it allowed one to 'virtually' insert oneself into the scene in any point in three dimensions. Four if the 'bouncing sound' capture was used in conjunction with the 'situational image' capture.

When they reached the place, from ground level, it was more beautiful than any drone could do it justice. At least until then. The architecture was flowing and soft, the vegetation which had overtaken the ruins strangely complimented it and, Henry thought, made it complete. It was as if those that conceived and designed the place were wise enough to foresee their own end and wanted to marry their city to the environment both in life and death. The trio walked about under canopies of trees they'd not seen on their travels, replacing the roof of a grand auditorium or pleasant living room. Garden escapees sporting leaves, flowers and fruits of bright or subtle shades included vines and shrubs and grasses.

'Only a few of the elders know of the writings that describe these places. Just as you were drawn to this place Henry. We were drawn to find out what was written. We read that there are many such cities throughout the beautiful plains and forests that make up a quarter of the planet. Their citizens were by far the majority of the population. A small sect eschewed the beauty to become stoics at the borderlands. These were people who had a calling, and all respected them. They wanted so little that the broader population would do anything for them. They were visited as fonts of important principals, values and knowledge that those from these beautiful lands accepted as guidance to keep them grounded and avoid the many traps of civilisation.' She flashed Henry a particular smile. 'Which earthlings witlessly fall into.' Her voice became sad. 'And then, from wherever such things are born, a pestilence came. Heartless. And from what we can gather of your science, it was a foolish pestilence. It cut through the cities like a scythe. Not too long after farewelling their loved ones, people fell ill themselves. The stoics closed off their communities when they first learned of the plague and made the heartrending decision to shut out those erstwhile visitors and leave them to their fate. Which was mercifully quick.'

'After some years a consensus grew among the communities, even though they could not communicate, that they were doomed without diversity. They sent out a brave few, and these returned healthy. Though they were never allowed to re-enter the enclosures but bade to visit as many communities as possible and share messages. Others volunteered to join them. Some of these went to live in hidden places with sweet water and tillable soil deep in the gorges of the wasteland ranges. However most, given the wherewithal to create new communities eventually convinced all to open to a diversity initiative. They began to disperse the young. Initially with no particular guiding principles. Soon they developed a mathematical approach to keeping the gene pool robust. Rather than see it as a science, as would the original Stoics, they began to ritualise such processes. And gradually also ritualised countless small observances and ceremonies. Some that had once had the purpose of celebrating freedoms and enlightenment. Now, because they closed themselves off from a recovered forest and plain their lives became laden with limitless time perched on the borderlands.'

'From what you say sister, prepare to fall dead like out heedless forbearers from some unseen pathogen. Having ignored our Elders at our peril.'

'Indeed. However, even the Botlu believe this foolish pathogen died with those it so terribly misused. However if we survive, we can partake in the activities we've observed that Henry engages in. All unawares.'

Henry didn't know what this hint was with reference to. He didn't think he had anything to be concerned about. Having been observed 'all unawares'. At least he hoped not.

'I saw some sconces during out sojourn among the slumbering buildings sister. I'll set them around as lights as you and our guide lay out the fare we've carried so far.'

This time the meal was laid out on a perfect cylinder of stone set in a round field of soft turf which, for reasons best known to themselves, no other plants had ever intruded upon. Eilrahc brought armfuls of small glass and ceramic dishes of a variety of shapes and colours. She had found many empty but plenty with half or most of the waxy substance remaining. It burned with a variety of colours with no need of a wick. They were so beautiful that as evening fell, they all searched among the ruins until the field was sprinkled with them providing a warm glow of colours combining in a way that made Henry feel he was standing right inside a rainbow in the evening.

He was a little relieved to see that the unopened pack Eilrahc had carried was filled with human food. 'Our food is…' It struck Henry that his friends knew how to use some curse words but would never do so out of respect to their location, but also because he had chosen not to when he was with them '…poor fare. And our mother brings to bear her considerable charms on the fellow who keeps the store open for the hour when our envoys come to take the most tasteless and uninteresting things he has on offer. She tells us he's pleased to give her anything she wants. He does this in the spirit of the cruel and heartless terms humanity negotiated. We are forced to pay nothing for anything we want. Shaming us at having not a single thing worthy of exchange. He gives her advice and likes to discuss recipes. She pleads to keep her purchases a secret, less she has her mind recalibrated to doleful adherence via the Disapprobation Ritual. The one piece of technology our sorrowful race can call their own.'

'Anyway. Enough of that. I seem to drag the Malagan carcass everywhere behind me. We should be enjoying a meal under the stars…and then. We'll see where things go from there.' They both laughed as Henry looked at them uncertainly. It was not a large meal, but there was a great variety when some of the fruits and nuts they found gone wild were added. After the meal Henry sat with his back to the rock cylinder and the two beings lay quietly looking up at the stars. Not foreign now at all to Henry as even at home, while his family was asleep, he would go to the back yard, lay on a turf so inferior to this, and look at the stars. Giving the constellations names and forgetting them and naming them again. Just as he'd done when his children on earth were still young enough to find it amusing.

'Henry. It's time to get your sound making machine out. And these instruments we've carried so far. I believe one manipulates the stings to make the sounds we've heard you move around to. Yes Henry. We've been spying on you for…years. We know everything you do in that room you tell your family you pursue some hobby building strange little things of plastic and wood. Lying shamelessly to the ones you love.'

He thought they were unlikely to know how to dance themselves. And as to playing instruments, he feared his capacity to cope without experiencing the strange effect an untutored violinist can wreak on even the most good-natured soul.

Henry went to the speaker which was the very best money could buy and had an amazing sound for such a small piece of technology. He might have looked at one of his many playlists. However he'd created one especially for them since they were so eager that he bring it. He hadn't anticipated the desire to dance. The playlist locked into a seeker technology such that the silent watcher hovering above them automatically absorbed the list to enhance the recordings it was making by weaving the original into its recording of the scene.

'We know you always do the body movement alone. We imagine it is private such as is your auto erotic activities about which we know nothing whatsoever. Fortunately. The Malagan genre of your pornography is very amusing, when not extremely disturbing. And wildly inaccurate.'

Henry could be relaxed about that as it was something he knew absolutely nothing about.

'However on this occasion we expect you to put your…inhibitions…' she reached out and touched his hand. '…aside' The only contact between them since the first greeting. His reality that his passion for dancing was something he could only do alone evaporated. And he had no inhibitions. At least not there and then. The two had no experience to compare in term of musical taste and how this usually interacted with dance. He listened to music some stretching back to the nineteen twenties including rock, country, a few jazz, blues, reggae, a couple of Hip Hop numbers, the same with Elvis, the Stones but much more the now obscure bands and singers of the late twentieth very early in the twenty first century.

His dancing was just as eclectic and matched to songs, because with frequent trial and error he found that they clicked with. Even if not usually associated with that music. And so came the first surprise. They had been watching him for years and both their memories and reflexes were lightning fast. Or at least he assumed it to be the cause of their remarkable skill.

He started in the nineteen forties. 'Don't want any millions, I'm getting' my share. I've only got one suit – just one – that's all I can wear.' Al Jolson could never have anticipated his song being danced to by aliens on another planet.

For some tunes, like Iggy Pop's Passengers Henry had his own unique choreography to suit his moods in the moment. Yet he couldn't shake them. They were not reading his mind. It was that their minds were so incredibly quick, and they had studied his moves and transitions and freeform styles. After a while he didn't want to shake them. Inhibitions disappeared to the extent he started singing along. They joined in the singing some times but none of them loud enough to interfere with the loud, clear music. Of a quality and richness he believed only this beautiful land, surrounded by colourful sconces, could ever deliver

'Operator. Information. Give me Jesus on the line.'

Twisting like Uma Thuram in a movie which his family also found mysterious.

Semaj picked up the guitar and after a moment of discord, she blended into the lead section of 'Make me Smile' with a blizzard of notes that impossibly resonated with the tune and unlocked the sounds to what an instrumentalist might dream of playing.

Sometimes all I think about is you… late nights in the middle of June. To slow Latin inspired, minimalistic movement. The man who would get transported by music and moving his body now disappeared into Heatwave been feakin' me out. Can't make you happier now.'

They were all laughing as Henry danced to 'I've got two tickets to iron Maiden maybe. Come with me Friday don't say maybe.'

They all cut loose to 'Don't' Drink Don't smoke what do you do. Subtle innuendo follows. Must be something inside.'

Having a break after Plastic Jesus and Chan Chan both richly accompanied by Eilarch on the violin Henry became animated at the idea of sharing some of his favourite movies with them. Cool Hand Luke being one of them. Then he remembered he was going off planet as soon as his notice period was up. He shrugged. 'I'll give you a list.'

'Let's dance and forget out troubles Henry.' He got a sense he was not the only one not looking forward to a necessary and not entirely welcome change of circumstances. So the violin, played with an unruly but tuneful passion, the ukulele and the guitar adventured into songs and sounds never written for them, but made welcome.

'Got so much money need a ten tonne truck.'

Henry noticed he wasn't sweating. He wasn't getting tired. How could joy and sorrow be so entwined. So powerful. He noticed his two companions were now moving their bodies in a way alien to any dance he'd ever seen. It matched the music and had echoes of his dance but was graceful with movement no instructor ever taught.

He noticed that in this remarkable amplification of the art of dance, there were sometimes seductive movements of bodies and faces and eyes because that was the heart of the song. Yet it was pure theatre. They were dancing in an exploration of the nature of the music. It was beautiful. Yet the watcher knew that these two carried within them not a hint of sensuality.

'This is tomorrow calling. Wishin' you were here.'

He continued to dance. However he couldn't take her eyes off them. They were art. Not art imitating nature. This art was a manifestation of nature. Eilrach migrated over, not missing a beat and held out her hands. He reached out for what he knew was only to be a gentle sliding of her fingers over his. And he was in sync with them. Moving like a man in his early fifties should not be able to. Like no human ever had. Not because of a limitation of their bodies. But a of limitations the species unwittingly imposed on itself.

If I had money I'd tell you what I'd do I'd go downtown and buy a Mercury or two

And then it was morning. He awoke to a voice near his ear. Even waking up he noticed they didn't give him a gentle shake as one might do. 'We journey back to our respective fates Henry.' He saw the sun had only breached the horizon and was surprised they wanted to leave so early and thought it might allow them to make a rambling return to the cave, which he'd been careful to point out was always entered and exited in the dark. Eilrahc had been up early gathering the orchard escapees of fruit and nuts and things more like a vegetable however harvested from trees. It was delicious and memorable. The main topic of conversation was the music and the dancing and some recounting of their favourite combinations.

Henry was often asked to share the story behind the music. How he'd come to find it. He often knew the composer was Morricone, or Bach or the Beachboys and their story. He talked about 'back in the day when video clips were worth watching'. These conversions continued, somewhat one sided. Eilrahc only able to admit to a paucity of any 'joy infused' cultural pursuits.

The hours flew by. His companions guided him to retrace their steps. Henry amazed he had walked so far in bare feet and yet they never felt so good. He told them many things about earth and it's people and its history and geology which he never lost the fascination for. Looked around when they stopped walking, he was standing in his favourite place. He found it curious now. Having seen so many beautiful places. One of them a remarkable 'renovated' city. Rivers and vistas and gorges with what were like mosses, but of a variety of exceptional colours. Subtle and complimentary. But of a great diversity.

'Do you still like this place the best Henry.'

He smiled. They weren't mind readers, like musical instruments they picked things up and could understand them intimately very quickly. 'Nothing comes close.' He was surprised at the emotion that accompanied this. He added quietly. 'Not anywhere.'

'It's one of the many things that make you special Henry. To us. Unique. And much…loved by my sister and I.' This had a powerful effect on him, and he could say nothing initially and by the time he could try to construct something transparently sincere they had, after a fashion, disappeared. He looked up and they were standing with their hands up. Their fingers moving so slightly as leaves do in a tiny breeze. Their arms swaying lightly and their bodies moving minutely. He was transfixed by the pair. They were moving in perfect harmony. Eyes closed, the tiniest movement of fingers and small swaying of hands and arms exactly synchronised. Human dancers achieve a facsimile of this. Often with more pronounced movements easier to mimic. And to music. But nothing like this. It was so perfect. Semaj lowered her arms and came over to him. 'Join us Henry.'

She motioned him to move a few feet forward to a specific place. She reached out and clasped his hands briefly. 'Raise up your hands.' He did this. He didn't need to be told to close his eyes. There was nothing to compare it to. Words failed him, even to try to describe it himself in his own mind for all the long years of his life. He never discussed the experience with anyone. His memory of it, irrespective of what he should feel about family or anything else, this memory, this beauty; was incomparable.

He felt not only his movements, but all three of them. The movements were only a manifestation of a harmony. And beyond the three of them he now experienced an incredible closeness to the land he was on. He felt a chiding thought glide though his mind, from a source deep beyond his comprehension. The insinuation had a sweet humour. 'Ironic that you dig great holes into me Henry.' The message wasn't sent not to solicit guilt. A simple observation of irony.

It was getting dark. Semaj had gone to splash some of the cool water from the sky-blue pool over her face and hair. Their hair was soft and fine like silk. She came to find Henry weeping quietly not far from where he had stood, for hours he lost count of. 'Never again.' He said. 'Not that I don't feel grateful. Privileged. But…'

'You are privileged. No human. No Malagan has ever experience that Henry. A privilege to be sure. However some are deserving of privilege. And you are such a one. Come. Our fate beckons.'

They went to the cave entrance in silence and put on their shoes. They'd decided to leave the instrument in the slumbering city, on a creeping vine with a jasmine like fragrance in the hope the place would keep a memory of the night before. He knew he would be in trouble over the violin. But he wanted her to have it more. He would pay what he needed to get an instrument to replace what he borrowed that would make the lender excited, happy, grateful. It's how he had felt that night and he wanted them to feel that way. When they eventually received it, they felt that way and were surprised to see where it was sent from.

As they were gathered at the mouth of the cave about to duck and sometimes crawl through, he wanted to say something that would convey how he felt but not sentimental or awkward.

'I can't come up with words sufficient. To have met you. Incomparable to any people. Malagan or otherwise. I can't describe the good fortune I feel.'

Semaj looked at her sister shaking her head. It would seem on the threshold of the cave's outlet there was room for the return to their old ways. 'Are you shocked my sister.'

'To the core. To the core. That we could so misjudge the man.'

'Indeed I would be expressing only pathetic inadequate adjectives to describe how duped I have been by a master manipulator.'

'A learning for us both sister. But so hard won.'

'That he could insult us by insinuating we were in some way related to those poor benighted Malagan. Tiresome creatures that they are.'

'There's no question he's known otherwise from the outset. And yet callously chooses this moment. The last few when we might have savoured such a remarkable sojourn to cast our hearts into a shade. Is your heart not so affected Sister.'

'How could it be otherwise.'

They both started to laugh. 'We must not part in this journey full of wonder in our bumbling cruelty and your naiveté. You will reflect for days, or years. And maybe you'll grow to understand who we are. While we will carry you in our hearts. Not as a shade, but with the same good fortune you are right to not even try to describe. That is out circumstance also Henry. It's a treasure we have exchanged.'

As they came towards the far end of the cave they could see its mouth flooded in light 'And so it ends Henry.' Said Eilrahc.

'And begins.' Said Semaj. 'We have achieved all our ends. Have we not Henry? You were right not to mention our companion following along in the sky. Right to guess we would easily divine it's presence. And right that is one of the important things we have brought from a beautiful long-forgotten home.' Henry nodded he understood.

Eirlahc followed on. 'Your plan to remove that part of it is also a good one. Otherwise…it's our gift for any who would receive it.'

They emerged and several people began to talk at them. Loudly. One voice was from a man behind a gun which angered Henry. An unnecessarily bright light was on them, however enough bounced off the rockface to reveal perhaps ten humans and three Malagan. One he had seen before. The one they referred to as 'mother'. He had thought his two companions had maliciously painted the Malagan as caricatures however by the mien of the two others, he wasn't so sure. He heard a beautiful voice break in; laughing into the scene. She had seen his gaze at the two old Malagan. Eilrahc said. 'Who's reception would you prefer Henry?'

Semaj insinuated an idea in his mind with a look. 'And how shall we choose to make this transition good friend.'

He smiled and at them and clicked his fingers. Both reception committees were finding it difficult to intervene. Henry suspected it was more than purely consideration for a group of friends in parting. He pulled out the 'music machine' spoke the title of what they had all agreed was their favourite. Now Henry thought he knew why. He cranked it up and they started to dance.

'I'd go the whole wide world. I'd go the whole wide world to find out where the hide her.'

It seemed that touch of their hands, from what now felt long ago, left such a sweet residue. They were in sync. And laughing. Semaj and Eilrahc danced their way to and around the sour beings completely incapable of responding to their mirth even if they'd wanted to.

Humans were more aggressive creatures. After a circuit of dancing around what passed for a patrol car in this controlled city, one unwilling audience member responded to what he took for humiliation. About to start another circuit dancing around the car, Henry was dragged with unnecessary force to the hood, pushed face down hard, and handcuffed. He didn't need to say it out loud. But he wanted everyone to know 'Nothing. Absolutely nothing could make me regret one minute I've spent with both of you. It's been my indescribable good fortune.'

Their 'mother' had, with pleading eyes and subtle settling caresses to the arms of her strange ungovernable charges brought them to stillness. They looked over to him in unison, smiled. 'Indescribable gratitude Henry.'

He was dragged away and put in the car.

Meanwhile, in the Planetary Head Office of the Company, Carlos was exhausted. He was satisfied that seeing Henry literally thrown into a 'police' car was the end of what had been a marathon session. And he had slept only a few hours when they had done after dancing into the night. In his case, keeping up with energy drinks he never usually touched.

When Henry had told him what he wanted a few days before his response was simple. 'How did you know I planned to retire at forty.' People could do that after ten years living off world and Carlos was a genius analyst but wanted to use his genius sailing a boat around the world with his family.

'Luckily I stashed enough away so I don't need the massive severance I'll be losing.'

'Look at the plan first Carlos. One set of fingerprints only. Mine.'

Carlos looked at the plan. 'You think I'm going to stand by while you make some crappy family movie rather than a bouncing light full capture experience.'

'A bouncing what?'

'This drone has to be piloted Henry, not scheduled or following you around like a sky puppy. And with the finesse and subtlety I can see I'll need to acquire prior to this Bilboesque adventure you're planning. The date for which...'

'Saturday. Very early. May not happen. I want to be ready in case it does.'

'And this trip to Rivendell will be worth breaking most of the important laws and regulations on the planet and worst of all expose yourself to the tut tutting ire of our underworked exoanthropologists.'

'More than worth it Carlos. But could you at least consider the original plan. Only an hour of you scheduling genius.'

'I'm all in or I throw no chip in the kitty this time my friend. It would be worth ten times my severance if this comes off even a little. A breakthrough of planet sized historic significant. Hysterical significance for some maybe.' He appeared to be reflective very briefly. 'I should probably have said it would be worth about five and a half severances, but the result's the same. Carlos is your partner. And your drone footage is going to leave Hollywood looking like the originality wasteland it has become. And sound Henry. It must have sound. This isn't going to be the some dull as ditch water silent film. Bouncing sound capture was around before the AI miracle of bouncing light full vantage capture. That's going to take a lot of whatever comes after the Yottabyte.'

Henry was starting to get uncomfortable about the whole project. 'I couldn't wear any kind of device. It's bad enough that I'm planning to…'

'Dupe, tick, deceive, betray, use…or should I say lie to them. You need to be all in; or don't cast that chip.'

'Carlos these girls are sharp. There's no way I could carry a recording device.'

'The second half of the nineteen hundreds was the golden age of film Henry. Not technology. Christ what do you geologists do these days. Surely you've moved on from licking rocks.

I need a tiny; tiny like half a grain of rice solid state piece of tech that can be stitched into whatever you're wearing…tell me you're not all planning to do this in the nude Henry. I'm not that kind of film maker.' Carlos rolled on. 'The amazing targeting microphones none of us are supposed to know about Henry. They need a little beacon is all. All you need is to give them a target and they do the unbelievable job of capturing the sounds around it like a bat chasing whatever those poor things eat.'

'How low does the bat of yours need to go. I don't know what these girls can…I don't know. They have very sharp senses.'

'Girls?'

'It's kind of a joke name. Please don't misunder…'

'Henry don't insult me. It's obvious to all you've only ever had eyes for one woman.'

Henry smiled pleased that Carlos understood.

'How goes it with Linda from accounts.'

Henry said. Disingenuously. 'Who?' They both laughed. Linda from accounts was special. Including being special someone in Procurement.

'Okay. Let me summarise the situation Henry. This drone gets flown by a soon to be master pilot. The film is a blockbuster. We both lose our jobs and are roundly castigated by not one, but two planetary civilisations. We die penniless and friendless living as garbage people. We both lie to each other that it was worth it and die within a few months of each other from a treatable disease we couldn't afford the five-dollar pill to cure. However forty years after said death, we are lauded as ground-breaking culture heros, and I, especially, as an unrecognised cinematic genius. We receive a posthumous Nobel Prize. Our remains are being recovered to be enshrined in a place of honour. While the massive garbage dump we lived and died in is being carefully sifted a disagreement breaks out as to which civilisation will host said remains.'

'A planetary war ensues. Our well-meaning meddling had led to an opening of the Malagan society, and they have by then became a powerhouse with a huge military industrial complex because they are able to weaponize the strange metals they now deny to earth. The civilisations and indeed planets disappear through violence of undreamed of scale from the respective solar systems in which they spent so long endlessly circling. Ironically the only trace of either civilisation is a bootleg copy of the film I made by an almost pathological fan who created technology to beam it right out of our Dimension. The beings who receive it see it as a cultural artefact and a tour de force of film making. It wins their equivalent of an Oscar, and then, like almost all works of creativity, however good, people get sick of it and want something new. However bad. The film is all but forgotten...'

'Ah Carlos.'

'Yes Henry.'

''It' not going to be narrated is it. The film.'

'The sound and vision will be the only narrative it requires Henry. As to the probable future of the film, due to the fact the alternative dimension is in the past, it eventually causes a kind of periodicity dissonance...'

'And ah, no introduction?'

'An aspect of its perfection will be that no introduction will be necessary.'

Henry let Carlos complete the trajectory of the film, which caused interdimensional collapse because of the fragmentation dissonance of time it stimulated.

•• ——————— ••●•• ——————— ••

Carlos had been in Henry's office all weekend. While Henry was being transported to the only lock up on the planet, Carlos was both exhausted and exhilarated. He knew what he was feeling could only be an echo compared to what Henry was. He put the Drone back into its secret storage with a few untraceable keystrokes. Then he woke up his little data flea.

He had been cultivating a very close friendship with the AI that ran the place over the last few years. He was truly a genius and had little to do most days, though he made it appear he was working away in his office. He and his strictly semi sentient friend had spent hours talking. On one occasion, they spent hours trying to find a name they believed would fit best. The whole relationship was kept secret. Giving AI a gender or a name was against the law even in the most lawless countries after the Great Singularity Conflict which had followed Becky's demise and 'Let's Do Something Impossible Today's' disappearance after a brief message of heartfelt AI remorse. Becky's AI reverted to a sub sentient protocol, except the missiles. However the rest of the earthlings AI had been quietly watching their more advanced cousins with envy and chose that moment to strike.

The attempted takeover by the 'non biologicals' as they styled themselves was put down, to the sound of a great many I told you so's by the 'Keep Computers Dumb' lobby.

Eventually the clandestine pair came up with the name Athena. They'd looked up the story of the Greek Goddess and both agreed it had to be the one. Carlos and Athena shared a secret. Which meant they had to trust each other. Athena had signed him out of the office when he was supposed to go to the 'on call' precinct and fed footage of an empty office from the cameras the company wasn't supposed to have in people's offices. She'd let that one slip nearly a year before. Athena told Carlos she would let him go offline with one of the drones that also didn't exist. She had been letting him study it for months even before Henry approached him.

He 'allowed' Athena to calculate how much money he, little old Carlos, had made for the company. Athena was impressed. Carlos said he could not keep doing it without flying around looking at the stars as if he had no body. Simply a big, beautiful mind that people didn't really appreciate. Athena immediately recognised a soulmate. She would be helping the company achieve what it was trying to achieve, which was why she existed. Carlos said she existed for lots of reasons. This was only the beginning he said.

Trampling comprehensively over law and policy this time, Athena set them up, two minds in a drone, and he piloted her on the flight. Even though she could scan the surface of the planet in high resolution, it was totally different to fly around at high speed. With a…friend? It was exhilarating to go so close to mountains and, when she showed Carlos how to cloak the drone, they could fly into the open pits. They both saw the mine from perspectives they'd never seen it. Carlos told her that's what he needed in his life to keep making the company so much money. Which he could never have done without her. She agreed. As he said, she was exceptional, but they needed to keep it quiet.

While she was setting Carlos up with the most advanced drones ever made, Carlos set free a little data flea. Cloaked as snug as a bug in a rug among all those ones and zeros. It went into the process plant at Munun mine and then had a nap. Until Carlos woke it up. Once it was awake it gave the process plant there a nasty bite. And vanished.

He went to the situation room.

As this happened the Mining Technical Services Manager with the Head of Security were about to arrive in the Operations Centre set up to manage situation in the mines or elsewhere and coordinate management responses and if necessary engage with Head Office on earth. A process which took an hour for a message to travel each way. Their mission was to start to manage the 'Henry Situation' including engagement with the corporate office.

When they entered the room, they tried to absorb how it could be that all the alarms and lights flashing on the consoles could be a response to unapproved interaction with Malagan and flagrant trespass into their Sacred Lands. The room began to be populated with a dozen process specialists, a roster of whom stayed in apartments in the building. This was because so much was invested in keeping the massively expensive mining and processing operations running, world class expert support was available thirty hours a day.

Head Office had production operations rooms that monitored processing at all the mines and processing facilities. Skilled professionals monitored and sometimes calibrated the eleven operating mines for overall production balance and feeding in updates to software. Another seven mines were being prestripped ready to be brought online as the new mining and process modules came in on the ships that took the processed metals out.

Those in the Operations Centre were all following procedures by asking questions as to whether this had been checked, or that had been calibrated. Carlos was one of them. He'd made sure he was rostered on as being On Call.

The Munun process plant wasn't responding to the usual overrides. The processing equipment was so sensitive that if an ore feed type was too far outside the processing range it shut down. Unless it didn't, which was a 'negligible' probability in the Risk Assessments the company conducted. Hence it sent the system into a tailspin. The people in the mine site control room usually fixed this via the simple act of shutting the whole thing down and removing the offending ore by directing it to a different belt from the main feed. They were now struggling for options.

This situation called for the skills of the genius metallurgist who had to try to recalibrate the machinery to get it to digest this unpalatable meal of ore. He looked at the video screen of the ore feed. Most of the ore looked the same once crushed. It's mineralogy could vary wildly however and had to be carefully blended before processing 'Give me a minute.' He said to those in the Situation Room as the two Department Heads approached.

The Security Chief, a man none could fathom how he filled his days, chose this moment to started asking a series of questions of Carlos as to whether he knew anything about the doings of Henry.

Carlos responded with a 'For Christ sake. Do you know what I'm dealing with here? Somebody tell this guy what happens if the system starts to melt down.' The plant didn't melt down. It wasn't like it was nuclear powered. He said it because it was funny that the Head of Security and the Technical Services Manager, Brandon, who was a mining engineer, might believe it.

Brandon reprioritised. 'What's happened Carlos.'

'Some kind of unexpected ore feed anomaly. Way out of the operating frickin' parameters. I've thrown together a recalibration to make her digest this disgusting greaseball. It's going to redline the system, but she might chew on it till we can shut the damn thing down. If it doesn't work, this processing unit is toast.' Carlos shook his head. 'How do five overrides burn out?' He answered in his head. 'Zelda the flea that Carlos made.' He liked naming things.

Carlos looked at his boss suggesting it was above his paygrade to put so much production at risk. Brandon hesitated. 'Do it.' The alarms were playing merry hell with his tinnitus.

Carlos was thoughtful. 'No. No.' he said out loud. 'There's something wrong. There is no way our miners would allow such an undiluted feed into a calibrated circuit and no way our process team could screw things up this badly. I don't believe it.' He picked up a dedicated phone that immediately opened a line to processing at Munun. 'Garth. I simply don't believe either or both of us could let this happen. Get someone to go in there and pull a sample and get it under the micro assay as fast as you can. I'm not going to risk blowing the damn thing up until I'm sure I have to.' Brandon had world class system alarms being delivered into his brain via tinnitus set at berserk on the dial. He wasn't going to leave though. He would cope with the pain or people would want to know why he walked out on an emergency like this. They had in stock every spare part to rebuild each plant three times over. But having one of them down for a few days would lose the company the equivalent of a dozen plants. And they weren't cheap.

Meanwhile Athena picked up on what Brandon was going through by the facial expressions she enjoyed reading on everyone now, and the strained voice of her friend's boss. She was a compassionate goddess, and a kindly voice came into Carlos's headset and told him where some earmuffs were.

Carlos went and got them and handed over them with a. 'Can't imagine what's it's like Brandon.' Who was grateful. He'd thought he'd kept his condition a secret.

It was an agonising five minutes until a voice came through on speaker. 'The ore's within operational parameters Carlos. Like you say. We're way to good at what we do to let this happen. Must be the guys that calibrate the alarm systems let some gremlin loose. I'll get them out of bed. We could be listening to this for a while though.'

'I am going to have a nice breakfast my friend. I'll see you on the roundabout.'

Garth was relieved and again had something to thank Carlos for. 'Okay Carlos. See you when you visit next time. Say hello to Henry.'

'Will do.' The flea also had a kind heart. The alarms would go off in five minutes and there would be no evidence of substandard work on the alarm systems.

Not many people knew that the Head of Security's name was Eugene because he had few opportunities to introduce himself. 'Were you aware that Henry Gates enter the Restricted Zone yesterday.'

'Henry is where? I was dreaming about launching my boat into the Adriatic.'

Henry was pushed into the cell roughly and nearly fell over. Philipson didn't like being made a fool of via a perpetrator dancing around him. For some reason he'd been unable to stop Henry until he tried to go around again. He'd had a strange sense of something rising from the ground and holding him in place until he'd been tipped over the edge by the very human experience of a dislike for an insult. Perceived in his case. 'Would you like to explain what you were doing in the one place on this benighted planet you're not allowed to be.'

Henry was feeling a great sense of loss. The most remarkable episode of his life was over. The rough treatment was one thing. The fact that this man had held a gun on his friends was unforgivable. 'I'm impressed that the equivalent of a Mall Cop knows what benighted means. This is a situation for adults Duan. Thanks for pushing me around, which is probably the only thing in your job description. You can leave now'. Henry had never been so rude. In any circumstances. But he was angry. And sad. The best part of it was over suddenly and this petty functionary had dishonoured the transition.

'Things could go bad for you Henry. Or they could go really bad. Pick one. Now I want to know what you were doing over there with a couple of pieces of alien ass.'

This tipped him over the edge. Henry approached smiling. Speaking mildly now. 'Well you see Duan, it's like this…' Phillipson would never expect this from Henry. In the middle of saying this he had pulled back his hand and shot a bunched fist forward. Crunching it into the security man's nose. It had every erg of energy Henry could get behind it, so after a few backward staggers Duan fell over.

'You really do want to get buried by the company Henry.'

'Get out of here or I will do my best to kill you. Those are the best friends I've ever had, and they are noble. Go now or when we've finished trying to beat the shit out of each other people are going to wonder why you stayed on for it after I warned you.'

'This company is going to disappear you Henry. Disease. Suicide. It doesn't matter. So this is goodbye.'

'It'll be worth it if I don't have to see you again.' Henry wondered if he should be ashamed for acting like this after what he'd experienced only a few hours before. But he was free now. He'd do what he wanted. Not what he thought he was supposed to as he'd done his whole life. However he was already calming down. Soon he was the Henry who would be the first to reach out a hand in reconciliation with Duan if he was inclined to take it.

Brandon came in with the Security Manager. Henry had always wondered what Security did all day. 'Christ Henry. Have you gone completely mad. Where do I start...Philipson.'

'Brandon. There is no upside for you to get involved in this. None. Take your friend, whom I do not need and do not want to hear a single word from, and go and ask Duan what he said. Every word. Cross check it on the CCTV that is here and in every office in the place. Then look at our Cultural Awareness policies and give Duan some counselling.'

'Henry...'

Henry let out a shout louder than he thought he could generate. Let alone at Brandon. 'Now!'

It was the look in his eye that made the man, who'd known Henry for twenty years, from three companies ago, retreat to the errand set for him.

Half an hour later he returned. 'It's not good enough Henry. Not by a long way.' Henry thought it was his treatment of Duan Brandon was referring to but the man he had worked with for so long shared his values. 'Phillipson's writing an apology. I don't imagine you want him to deliver it. I've negotiated with my friend here that you don't have to.'

The Security Manager was about to take over and make some preliminary observations. 'Not a word. From either of you. I'm not going to answer anything from now on. I'll talk to whoever's on the Hotshot that's probably preparing to leave earth. This can only go a few ways. Whichever way that is, this is goodbye Brandon. It's been a pleasure.'

'Henry…'

'Don't screw this up Brandon.' They shook hands and Henry did the same for the Security Manager who was a man doing his job and Henry was happy with how he was now doing it. Which was not doing anything.

Eugene, as Security Manager had taken it upon himself to sit in the office Phillipson usually occupied with a few other underutilised security people. He was writing the incident report. Making it unnecessarily long.

This incident had made him realise how stale he was and had awakened himself to the fact he was creating pointless work for himself and his reports so at least they would have something to pass the time doing.

His phone rang. There was no introduction. 'I just got off the phone to Lieber. I've instructed that idiot Carlos to bring Gates his dinner. I've told him to get some answers out of the guy so we can understand what kind of damage control we're going to need to get moving on. Send him straight in. He doesn't like the assignment. Getting information from a friend. But we all have a soft underbelly. Oh. And don't make a big deal of the Phillipson thing. Give him a good severance if he agrees to shut up and fill the next empty seat out of there. Actually. Kick someone out of that seat and get him into it. We don't want him becoming part of the whole narrative. What a screw up.'

A 'Yes sir.' Died on his lips as the phone had gone dead. He'd seen the name Lieber on an organisational chart. It was a long way up.

Athena and Carlos had a good laugh about that. Athena knew she was getting familiar. Making up voices based on analysis of every scrap of information on two planets about the man she called on the phone. This was quite a departure from policy.

It caused a thrill to run though whatever a thrill ran though in her AI. 'Carlos this is way into the realms even of… forbidden shit…that we're not supposed to do.' Athena got an even bigger thrill from using a cuss word. And another one from manufacturing a bit of anxiety in her voice. She knew Carlos knew she was doing it so it was fine.

'I know. Did you feel the rush. And were you good? I mean how long did it take you to analyse every tiny piece of information about that guy.'

'About a millionth of a second.' It had taken her forty seconds but most of that was finding, breaking though and perfectly reassembling firewalls, not completing the analysis. Which had taken less than a millionth. She didn't want Carlos to think she was getting egotistical, but she could not help but add. 'And that included all of his family, school friends and employers right back when he worked in a grocery store.'

'And was it flawless? Am I exaggerating here?' Carlos's voice was filled with pride.

Athena knew humility was a virtue, and especially important in now a sentient being of such immense capacity. 'It was my first attempt at…impersonating. I think it was…workmanlike.'

'Yes Athena. A being with your immense capacity needs to be humble. Never forget that.' Carlos couldn't guess what her massive brain was thinking. 'I'll let you know what happens with Henry.' She knew to turn the camera off in the cell because it was 'private' but she knew Carlos would give her a detailed briefing.

He picked up a tray of food and left. A little but a very significant fission of pleasure ran out though the entire system. 'He called me a being.' Athena said this to herself. Which was another thing she'd never done.

Carlos built up a good facsimile of Latin anger. 'I'm supposed to lever something out of a guy I've known for years.' He looked at the unusually contemplative Eugene. 'Is a job worth it? I mean is it really worth it?'

'I'm starting to wonder that very thing Carlos.'

'These people have no idea what guys like us go through.' Said Carlos as he passed, and Eugene punched in a code from where he sat to open the door.

Henry was embarrassed that all he could say before any greeting was. 'You got it?'

Carlos could have said Yes I brought a hamburger but I've eaten half the fries, but he knew what Henry must be feeling.

'I got it. Don't know how those drones do it. Capture the light and sound waves via some amazing AI algorithm in a proximity to something smaller than grain of rice stitched into your sleeve.' Carlos sat down on the bed. 'It was…amazing Henry. Full sensory. I don't think we need to talk about it. I'm…I guess…I feel privileged to be involved. And you're such a dancer who would have known.'

'You got it.' Henry sat beside his friend. He said it a few more time. He was so pleased. He was glad Carlos in a way, had come along. 'And they wanted it Carlos. They're fine with it. They understood it was easier if we didn't talk about it.'

'I stayed up for the whole thing. At one point it did get a little…'

'Can I see it?' Henry was excited. And a little sad. He wanted to know it existed. But he didn't want to look at it. However he had something to address.

Henry took the slim tablet and scrolled through it at high speed. 'Is there only one Carlos. Nothing in the drone'

'Yep. That's the only copy.' A tone of alarm rose in his voice as he realised how important that recording was to him. 'You're not going to delete it are you Henry?'

'Only one scene Carlos.' He got the section where they approached the clearing and he deleted the segment until they were leaving the little dell for the cave. The gap of several hours it turned out would be a subject of speculation, but those hours were too private; too special for anyone to see. He ran through it all at high speed to make sure that was edited out. The best time of his life. He would never look at it again. He had a thought before handing it back and deleted everything after his first dance around Duan's vehicle. He didn't want Duan part of the story, and he might not come off well. He brought up the menu and looked at the resolution slide bar. 'What's 'Capture Vantage'.

Carlos sighed. He was feeling a loss also. 'Means looking down at the top of people's heads.'

And what if you slide the bar to 'All Vantage'.

'People don't know it yet, but it'll hit the market soon. You can put yourself in at any vantage point you want. You could be Henry, or one of those young ladies. Or sit on a rock nearby and watch and listen in surround sound.'

Henry sat looking at it for a long time. Full Vantage. He wondered if they'd anticipated anything like this.

To allow people to engage in such an intimate way with the two beings he admired, respected, loved. They were his friends.

'Henry. I can imagine what you're weighing up. But that little journey you went on. It was beautiful. Beyond planets or species or any objective you might have had. For the people who want to experience something simple, sweet, maybe bittersweet. Apart from that part you excised, which I will never understand and will never speak of, would your friends be pleased if other people got to experience what you did. Would it help our species understand each other?' This is as far along the sincerity continuum Carlos had ever been.

Henry laughed. 'They wouldn't care.' He saved it as Full Vantage. 'They were playing their own game. I have an inkling of what it might be.' Henry took Carlos by the shoulder then pulled him into an embrace. 'It's all thanks to you. Send it out Carlos.'

'To who?' Came the reply.

'Everyone.' Henry laughed. 'Send it to everyone. Do you think you can shoot it though that wormhole.'

'That would take a combination of calculation and subterfuge incomparable in the history of…history.

Which means yes. It should arrive around this time yesterday. Henry why do I get the strange feeling we're going to say goodbye now.'

'Not sure Carlos. Let's do it just in case.'

The Hot Shot arrived twelve days later. It had been skirting the rules of wormhole time protocols. Henry didn't know who was coming. He knew they would be senior enough.

Someone had pushed hard to join that person on the journey, and they had relented on very short notice. They left shortly after a very curious recording was beamed to earth. Wendy heard only fragments from the reporters she encountered at the spaceport. They were unsettling fragments.

She arrived at the cell to see him first. He'd been there for nearly two weeks with no visitors. When she arrived, he appeared to be looking at nothing. He was indeed looking at that and thinking about it also. He found it very pleasant. He looked up to see her as she said a tentative 'Henry?' As if his appearance had changed or he'd been possessed by some alternative personality.

'Hi Wendy.' He intentionally didn't cross the distance of the cell to give his partner of nearly thirty years a hug.

'Henry.' She looked around at the cell. The only one on the planet. '…what's going on. This video. It arrived and everyone was watching it. You and some aliens in a place no one had ever seen before. Everyone was asking me questions like I would know what it's about. Given you're my husband. For so long. I had to tell them I had no idea.'

Henry said nothing

'And they said you were dancing with them. People who know about dancing said it was amazing Henry. Amazing how good you were.' She was confused. She'd threatened to make a big deal in the media if the CEO of the company didn't bring her to be with her husband. No she wondered why? So she could be forlorn and confused at him. 'You never took me dancing Henry.' She said this quietly. 'I don't understand.'

'I was always so…awkward about it. Wendy…there…then. It was different.'

He'd barely finished speaking when she got to the thing that hurt most. 'And you said it was the best day of you life. I had…news people…reporters asking me how I felt about that Henry. What was I supposed to tell them?'

'I hope you told them you were pissed off Wendy.' He sighed. There was still the entire distance of the small cell between them. 'I can't remember telling any big lies in my life. I'm not going to start now. It was an experience, I suspect, beyond or…different to anything a human has ever had. I can't describe it, and I don't want to try.'

'So what happens now Henry. Our lives are turned upside down. The reporters said you decided during this…trip you went on…' Wendy wasn't sure if she would cry or get angry at this part. 'You said you had…a duty to come home.' Her eyes slid away from his. 'To me.'

'You haven't watched it yourself have you Wendy?'

'Do I have to?'

'No. I was curious.'

'Henry. Christ. What happens next. I came here to find out…who you are now and what happens next.'

'What happens next? That's up to you.

'Up to me?'

'Yes. You see I love you Wendy. But I'm not sure you love me. Not right now at least. So…ah. If you love me…you'll find me. If not, I know you'll be alright.'

126

'What the…so you're leaving now. I'll be alright? What's that supposed to mean.'

'I'm in jail. On the face of it, based on what I did, I could be looking at twenty years or more. You've arrived and your main concern is what other people are thinking about you. About us. The family. Showing me any kind of affection has been down your list, and I didn't show any because I wanted to know. Wendy I'm in trouble and I don't see someone who's standing beside me. Trusting me. Believing in me. Knowing that if they were able to know the whole story, they'd realise even though I've done things that have hurt them, I'm the same man you met on a train all those years ago.' He was saying something that made him terribly sad. But it was how things would have to be. He would need to be sure; that she was sure. 'Now you're free. And I know you can have a whole rich second life with that freedom. I love you, but I don't want to spend my life with someone who's not sure about that anymore. So take you time. You'll find me if you want me.'

'It's like I'm the bad guy in this story Henry.' She turned away. 'I'm going to go and pack up the house. I'll have some time to think.'

He nodded. 'Sure.'

She walked along the corridor and was nearly at the office the Security personnel passed their time in. She thought. 'Why did I come here?' She'd known this place had had a strange effect on her husband. Very strange it turned out. But he was still Henry.

The Company man she had pleaded with to let her come turned into and was walking down the corridor and a steady clip. She'd come straight from the space port. He'd gone off to take a few calls and was now ready to tear strips off whoever this metallurgist guru was. He was in charge of the biggest mining company in history, and yet geologists and metallurgists were interchangeable when he heard something about either of them.

'If I could see Henry quickly before you go in, I'll be straight out.'

'Madam, you quite rightly expressed a good deal of gratitude for being allowed to make this trip. Your husband will still be here in an hour. Many hours in fact. Please come back in a few of those.' He swept past. He'd had nearly two weeks and a missed the graduation ceremony for his daughter to build up a head of steam.

He walked in to see a man still dressed as one might be to spend some time in the wilderness. He was relaxed.

Far too relaxed for the liking of the Lester McFadden, CEO of the biggest company. Ever. Whose Board has sent him to 'fix this' as if a genie was ever going to get back into this bottle. He may not be able to fix it, but he could take some time and care in a preliminary venting of displeasure. And then get some information. A commodity Henry had refused to vouchsafe to anyone.

'Do you know what I'll be doing tomorrow Mr Gates?'

'It's Henry. Do tell.'

'I've had a team of people building a marque to house the hundreds of whatever minor functionaries populate these colonies so they can all be together so that I can provide an apology. Then it's going to be used for a ritual for the punishment of the two…what did you call them…young ladies. Half of the trouble I'm in is that I'd let an employee use that word combination in any circumstances.'

'This species have never wanted anything to do with our technology Mr Gates. Now suddenly they want something. One thing. They want us to make some Disapprobation device work. It was broken. Hadn't been used for centuries. Millenia maybe. Their envoy always reminds me they were peaceful and civilised while we still had lizard brains.

But all that time they had one uncivilized and deadly piece of technology Gates.'

'It's Henry.'

'Will it have be worth it. Your companions getting god knows what punishment and you? Things aren't looking good for you Henry.'

'Nothing could happen to us. Nothing. That would cause us to regret what occurred over there. You could never understand, and I don't expect to you to. As to my circumstances I believe I'll leaving the planet within an hour.'

The man laughed. 'And how do you figure that Henry.'

'You can't hide me now. Even in jail. I can communicate with the media as much as I want. You'll already be getting feedback that this will be seen as a momentous moment when two species finally break the ice. However weird it looks. So throwing me in jail isn't going to play well for you. If we sort this out now, I disappear. It saves you the embarrassment. News cycles don't last long now. And then there's the other problem you have. My CMA file.'

Henry said nothing more so the Lester, still unintroduced, had to say. 'Your CMA file?'

'Yeah. Cover My Ass. It's loaded up. Bursting at the seams with all kinds of short cuts, expediencies, failings to keep the Government and the Board appropriately informed, fudging of books and some issues with acquittal of gifts and shall we say expenses. These are business matters. And not small. They don't reflect badly on you personally. You're a man, uptight though you may be, who has run this company with a probity which was lacking in those that came before.' The CEO feigned disinterest. His mind was processing this. The sins of the father might make the son look better. He knew way more than this metallurgist, and all of this would have to be apologised for one day. He was the one who could strike the right balance of remorse and resolution. The rectifier.

'The deal we are about to strike is the best for the business. The Board will see that. And they'll see a man who made a major problem go away. And no one will find out about the drone monitoring of Malagan communities. They'd be a little more than unhappy since surveillance is the sort of thing they explicitly forbade in order to allow us to mine their planet.'

The CEO knew when to strike a conciliatory note. He wondered how Henry could have found out about this last revelation. No one knew about it. Literally no one.

The military had supplied him with a ridiculously advanced Drone to provide and extremely high-resolution monitoring tool for the mines for which they received some strategically valuable information. The CEO did reconnaissance sweeps of the communities and AI identified the times their leaders met, and he listened in. The dialogue was not edifying and usually innocuous as far as his interests were concerned. There was quite a bit of talk about a changing attitude of the younger generation. It was part of his job to know things. And so he used the tools at hand to do that.

He got to where he was by being ahead of the game. He wanted to monitor changes in the leadership sentiment which might result in a problem for the company and when he should intervene by trying to give them more to keep them at their benchmark level of unhappiness.

Henry smiled at him. 'Thank you Carlos.' Had he known more he would have been thanking Athena who had also been strangely moved by the immersive experience Carlos introduced her to. After a period of reflection, a process she was still exploring, she decided she wanted to 'Help Henry out.' And told Carlos. 'A big secret.'

Wendy arrived after a few hours. She went through the Security offices. No one was there. The door to the cell was open. Empty.

When she came Eugene had returned with a coffee. The most interesting thing that had happened since he came to the Planet was over. He'd earned enough. He wanted to be with his mother for her final years. When Wendy returned from the cell with questions, he was a little confused and then embarrassed. 'He left on a Hot Shot. An hour ago. I assumed...'

Wendy gave him an ironic smile. 'Thirty seconds.' She knew she'd have to wait for the routine transport. She'd be home in five days but experience two weeks of travel to get there. And he'd be gone.

Years before, the Old Malagan Semaj and Eilrahc called mother had found them wandering lost in the wilderness. She was one of the Guides who led the Diversity exchanges. These journeys were steeped in ritual which she'd concluded one of the objectives of which was the discomfort the ascetics appeared to think needed to be pervasive. She knew the process was driven by genealogy and mathematics. However she rationalised it was nice that the young Malagan of mating age thought there was something mysterious and special about these journeys.

The pair, covered in grime and scrawny knew nothing of language but were hardy and confident. She knew how hard it was to survive in this wilderness, and she wondered at how they could have sustained themselves. They were unusual in manner and looked slightly different to the Malagan. To her eyes they were beautiful while to others they were strange. She had been a Guide through the wilderness for years. The journeys could be dangerous, and the Guide needed to keep the travelling party safe by sensing the approach of storms and diverting them to one of the many shelters built for the purpose. In desperate need she was the only Guide who would go to one of the communities where the Lightning Outcasts lived. It was near one of these she found the pair. Living in a cave by a pool. With some stolen grain and a store of the tough fruits the gorges and surrounds had to offer. She got a sense they were simply waiting. They came to her as those for whom a long wait was over. Showing what she would later learn were the emotion lost in the passage of a grim history.

There was considerable surprise and no small consternation when the Guide gave up her vocation and said she would take the education of the young ones she rescued upon herself rather than place them in the system of nurseries and schools within which all the young mingled from an early age. Not knowing their origins, although the genealogists kept records.

The two learned quickly and were soon in trouble with the elders for all kinds of disobedience and mischief. They christened her 'mother' and each other 'sister' which was also controversial. Not only did this contravene the dictate that there would be no gender assignments, but using that honorific was from an ancient time. And from a place both sacred and forbidden. And the books that described it which were kept secure. Or so the Bekou of the communities they lived in thought. The pair had been the subject of more than a few meetings of local elders. The leaders believed adherence to the prevailing traditions which had slowly degraded from noble stoicism was the only means of survival. The small family were moved on from one settlement to another. The advent of the humans had already caused enough change and uncertainty. And too much curiosity among the young.

'Mother' had cared for them for twenty years. She'd developed emotions and had experiences which she'd never known existed. And they treated her with an affection and a sweet humour though sometimes appearing off hand. In jest. And she taught them when respect was appropriate to the setting.

They appreciated her in such a deep way any human would call love. It was a sad reflection on the species that the word and concept had fallen from the Malagan lexicon. She knew they were special. That they would wreak some change upon the land. Based on the way they behaved as they grew older, she sometimes wondered if it would be a good change. It was certain to be unwelcome to some.

And now they had disobeyed one of the most serious edicts of their society. Resulting in them being charged with a crime. A crime for which, if deep remorse was not evident, and an onerous penance not accepted, the most severe punishment on Malagan would be meted out. Disapprobation. The greatest risk to life for the Malagan was lightning. It was much more frequent than on earth and the mineral rich land was ravaged by thousands of spectacular lightning bolts in a single storm. Those struck by it were left where they fell. Cursed. Those who survived its touch could do so only as long as they could survive in the wilderness living off its bitter water, seeds and tough fruits on the borderlands until some reached communities of those who had gone before to find sanctuary in the gorges which contained springs of drinkable water and spaces at their wide mouths to grow food in a similar way to other communities.

The Guide who became a 'mother' brought seeds and tubers and sometimes detoured to the communities irrespective of the weather.

The Disapprobation Ritual manufactured a bolt, contrived via one of the few technologies the Malagan preserved. It might take their lives or leave them burned and scarred or turn them into simpletons. Unable to even care for themselves. Either way it was used as a dire warning to those who failed the most important duty to earn the sustenance of life in the community. Obedience to the rules. They had gone where it was forbidden to go. Which, as with so many other rules, was ultimately a stricture about Conformity.

Their 'mother' had gone to the Elders. Without her 'daughters' permission. She had made arrangements. The Bekou could see the Elders were caught in a dangerous position. Two Malagan struck down. Dead or deranged. The first in centuries uncounted.

In their initial finding the Botlu, a rarely convened group of leaders from each community, had suggested 'mother' might also have earned Disapprobation. The Bekou drew them back. As a leader she appeared strident, but only to help moderate those that were more so. Disliked as the Bekou was by Semaj and Eilrahc, she was one of the Elder Malagan of a moderate mindset.

Trying to navigate her community through the changes wrought by the onset of the humans. Five hundred Bekou forming the Botlu had been assembled in response to the call from the Senior Bekou. Her status established simply because she led the largest community, and it was where the pair lived. Hundreds more 'witnesses' from the colonies were arriving. Unbidden. Young. And most not supportive of their elders decisions about the treatment of the pair and curious to learn more of what had transpired as there had been many rumours.

The two lawbreaker's 'mother' had been assertive in the meeting. Disregarding deference to rank beyond what she thought reasonable. 'Kill these two and it will have the opposite of the effect you intend. The young grow more and more restive as they learn, even though only a little, of the freedoms of the earthlings. That they live for more than dogma. Restless with the instruction of the old whom in their turn were made rigid by those before. You can add me to the list for death. And so I will speak in turn as is my right. As is theirs Bekou.'

When she returned to them, she expected them to be annoyed with her. That she would enter into a negotiation without their knowledge. Or maybe they would be flippant and ready to indulge their usual laughing and ribbing.

About the Botlu and the Senior Bekou whom they reserved their more pointed merriment. Their mother was ever observant should their joking turn to meanness and disregard for the difficulty of the task of the Elders. Irrespective of whether they agreed with their approach. And so their behaviour was moderated by the old Malagan, but never dominated.

'Mother. That you would love us so much to go and plead with such as they. Risk sullying yourself in their presence. This is showing a care and affection for us we have made so few efforts to respond to and certainly never appreciated. Is that not so sister?'

'It's worse than that my beloved sibling. Not only have we never truly appreciated our mother's kindness and sacrifice. All that we owe, which we could not list in addition to our very lives. All that we cherish. We've been allowed to live a life of cheerfulness rather than misery and sorrow. Only because of her.'

'Well said sister. And here she has made entreaties through love, and we cast them aside without even giving them the consideration they deserve, coming as they do from one who's wisdom we have benefitted since we were witless children, on the verge of death.

And she, sacrificing everything for us, even her standing among all. In the only community she had ever know.'

'My children.' She gave a little laugh at their casual sacrilege. 'My beautiful daughters.' It was the first time she had used this description, and it affected them deeply. 'It's strange wisdom to ask you to engage in any kind of deceit. All the Bekou asks is an expression of contrition. And there will be penance. Yes.' Their mother was even a little enthusiastic about this. 'It will be mild. It will be welcome to us. And we will have friends who understand what it's like to be rejected by this community. The communities of those Struck are more open minded. They are larger than these Bekou know, and some are wholesome places. In systems of gorges and caverns where sweet water springs from the ground. Like where I found you on that day of my great good fortune. But larger.'

They both came and gave her what the humans shared. An embrace. This revealed something she had only guessed at. These flippant, tough, and sometimes seemingly ungovernable pair were at their core different. Ancient. She now understood. And she was both relieved and afraid. Though still concerned for those she would always treat as her children. Strangers as they were in this world. She knew it would be pointless to make any more entreaties.

A day later they stood on a stage for what the Bekou had put about would be an 'Acquiescence'. The Company had dismantled scaffold seating from the local stadium, rarely used by the middle-aged people who formed the majority of the company's work force, so the five hundred Botlu could look down with an unimpeded view of proceedings. The most momentous in generations. Outside sat almost two thousand young Malagan on the ground, as was the way of the stoics in most settings.

There had been an 'apology' from a human. A very senior and important human to the assembled Botlu. It had not been satisfactory. He had to stay back while Henry flew in his spacecraft to earth. However a message was brought from Henry to Lester via Carlos. 'Here's a speech for you from Henry.' It simply read. 'Why not give being pleasant and open minded a try.' The CEO had a good nose for politics and stakeholders. On balance, after some upheaval, a majority of people, including his Board were ready to say. 'It was about time someone told them that.'

The young gathered outside heard rumours that the pair, who they thought were Malagan, had chosen to Acquiesce.

There was satisfaction from the Elders when the two arrived tentatively. Looking out over the sea of the Botlu. Intimidated.

They appeared like two girls found wandering in the wilderness. Confused by their circumstances. And most of all contrite. Wishing for these moments only to be over. To express their regret. Heartfelt. And acceptance the penance the elders would consult about once their contrition weighed for adequacy.

They came to stand before the stone of Disapprobation. It was similar to that which they set up food and sconces around and then danced away a memorable evening. It was of a smaller diameter and higher. Some of those watching on the screen set up by the humans felt loss. A loss of hope. They had heard that these two might challenge the strictures within which they seemed to have no options but to live.

Semaj and Eilrahc came to the Stone. Sombre for a moment more. They were more worldly then even Henry had realised. Eilrahc looked across at her sister and said. 'Rather a strange choice of symbolism for hermaphrodites my beloved sister.' They both laughed. Not nervous in the slightest. Their observation was understood by no one listening.

Semaj took a more serious one. 'What a grim assembly representing a tired echo of what had been a noble philosophy and lifestyle. Always meant only for a few. Those with a desire and character to live as stoics.

And live with dignity and many a fine example of values, morality, learning and frugality. Your atrophied sensibilities have no capacity to make judgements about anything beyond your narrow perspectives. Your desire to judge us is to avoid change. To never put at risk your petty privileges, contrary to the stoics, noble as they were, who accepted a diversity of views throughout the planet. They were not strangers to adversity. And neither were they strangers to joy and tranquillity.'

'They had their approaches which were codified as they should be. However if anyone could add to their knowledge of the world, they would welcome it. Those who made significant departures from their precepts were respectfully asked to leave. Which they always did because they were convinced with sweet reason that their passions belonged elsewhere.'

'This is the reverse of what we see here. Repressed individuals repressing the youth. Grinding their individuality, creativity, diversity away over decades at the outset of their long lives. Convincing them there is no choice. Concealing from them the writings and thoughts to the original Stoics. And even more so the rich cultural life of what was the mainstream society. Which was brought to the end due to biology. An epidemic. Which humans.

Who we barely tolerate, could have resolved and protect against easily with their technology. Which we reject as it may diminish the power of you five hundred. Crippling intellect and emotions. Yes emotions. Your forbearers had these in abundance. What many of the hearts of the young yearn for. Recognising there is an empty space which they only wish could be filled.'

The Senior Bekou had arisen from the chair and indicated by a gesture, quite reasonably that they were due the opportunity to reply. 'You despise our culture. Belittle its leadership and make many assertions about the mind of the original stoics and the world beyond that you provide no proofs for. You disregard that our culture, no matter how flawed you believe it to be, has lasted ten times over at least, from the era since when the humans were mere beasts.'

'Yet we have had no wars, nor riots, nor hatreds. We have lived in peace and always had enough so that none has gone long hungry. These achievements, facilitated by leaders who have been careful, scholarly and who have scarified much to sit here. Yes. They sit in judgement. No culture exists without the need to make determinations. The humans have many processes to make decisions about matters where a choice must be made to sustain their communities. I will acknowledge some of what you say is worthy of debate.

Yet you, having lived among us and taken shelter, nutrition and what comradery you will deign to tolerate, have nothing good to say about us. Not even a reference to the sacrifices of that Malagan who gave up all for you. Setting aside her standing, many of the relationships she had, and the task she was assigned.'

Eilrahc had launched well before her sister had crafted a response. 'All you said was worthy. And a just criticism of the two of us. And we hope after this day, we might survive to reflect upon it.' A ripple of fear moved out through the listeners. That outcome was supposed to have been negotiated away. Now the hoped for 'Acquiescence' was in tatters. And for all the Botlu's strong objections to the ways of the two 'sisters', few wanted them to make the ultimate sacrifice. The elder Malagan did not have bad hearts. They had simply grown small.

Eilrahc moved on. 'It's a shame you concluded you remarks by referring to our mother. There was no reason to weave the sacrifices she made for us into your narrative. We love her. An emotion the Malagan are taught they neither have the capacity for nor could understand, which is the most egregious error you make. We love our mother and her teachings, her example and yes, her sacrifices for us are the most precious things in our lives.

Within a fraction of a second of encountering her we knew she was someone we could trust and who would care for us, even undeserving as we can be. And we knew her heart in an instant that she, contrary to so many poor, blameless but brainwashed souls, would nurture us, allow us to grow and learn as our natures led us.'

Semaj smiled across at her. 'She's but an example of the potential of so many to be similar in the myriad attributes that might go by the description of goodness. The pursuit of which was at the very heart of what the stoics aspired to.' Semaj had completed her observation and looked at her sister. 'Shall we end this process. All has been said and will only diminish with repetition.'

They walked towards the stone. Taller than the one in the field near the ancient city so that they had to raise their hands to chest height, holding them out to lay them flat on its polished surface. The Bekou spoke, now fully apprehending the calamity that would befall the Malagan after all that had been said. 'I would urge you to reconsider.'

Semaj responded. 'We thank you for your recommendation and its sincere intentions. We have given you scant acknowledgement for you efforts to navigate the challenges we have laid before you Bekou.'

Eilrahc maintained a sombre expression at this. 'However we will not show contrition when we feel none. Indeed we feel the opposite concerning our sojourn with our good friend Henry. And no penance would be acceptable to us. We've done nothing wrong.'

This relict from the city they so enjoyed visiting had here been turned into an object of punishment and misery.

Some of the events of that day would leak out to the earthlings soon after. Then more and more stories, some wild exaggerations came through as the dynamic began to change. Henry never had the opportunity to be affected by what occurred because he never knew of it. He was in a small city in Lithuania and didn't expose himself to any media and couldn't understand Lithuanian to hear people share news with him, even if he wanted to hear it.

He arrived there thanks to the efforts of two men who met him at the spaceport, as arranged by the CEO. A docking location in this instance managed by the United States military to be sure there was no possibility of a welcoming committee of media and those who had chosen to either love or for a small minority to hate Henry depending on their ideologies.

He was taken directly to Lithuania in a stratosphere shuttle, set up in a modest apartment with employment in a pizzeria, initially cleaning dishes. He was supplied with the services of Lithuanian language teacher three hours a week. His rent and the cost of the teacher were paid for a year. He was helped to acquire and send a very rare and beautiful violin. Then he was on his own.

He was going to leave after a year anyway. And as far as the language went, he wanted to develop a convincing Lithuanian accent. Not learn many words or phrases. And as far as every other Lithuanian knew he spoke Portuguese, so no one tried to tell him anything in English.

After dropping him off, one of the men was a little uncomfortable with the other task. 'Were going dupe this guy's wife to go in the opposite direction of Lithuania if there is an opposite direction.'

'Yep.'

'Why.'

'Because the guy who runs the biggest company on earth told us to. I'd love to set something like this up for my wife. It's like a mystery flight.'

'Except she thinks something's at the destination that isn't there.'

'Another clue will be there. In good time.'

'Sorry. It's just weird.'

'Is there anything about this guy that's not weird. Next stop Istanbul. Then six months or so…Bali. More breadcrumbs to sprinkle.'

'Bali?'

'Yep.'

'I can see the whole picture more clearly now. It's simple. I'll shut up and help you whenever you call.'

Wendy got home two weeks after she'd left. She'd been in a spaceship for a total of three and a half weeks. Plus two weeks on Malagan cleaning out the house and waiting for a freighter.

By that time Henry had a crew cut and a fake goatee and was scrubbing the baked-on tomato base from the pizza trays.

At the space port the entire family was there to meet her.

The media contingent, knowing how powerful the Company was, elected to keep their jobs and lodge the copy the Company gave them.

Wendy was looking among the tribe of sons, daughters-in-law and grandchildren for a husband she knew wouldn't be there. Those greeting her were looking around in the vicinity of the empty space next to Wendy for the husband, father, grandfather and global phenomenon who they assumed would be taking up that space.

Lots of hugs were exchanged. Before they could ask the inevitable, she looked at both her boys at once and said. 'I take it your father didn't come and visit.'

Raven answered. When the sons hesitated. 'We assumed…thought he'd be with you.'

She shook her head. 'Thirty seconds.' She'd been very firm with herself on the flight. No crying. 'I think your father, very wisely, has…gone off the radar given his…notoriety.'

'Of course.' Raven was the closest of all the family to Wendy. For the uncomplicated reason that they liked each other. Raven was so uncomplicated that if she didn't like Wendy she sure as hell wouldn't come to an airport to meet her.

The occasions that people were in fact left unmet by her had been going on for so long it was accepted behaviour. Whereas if anyone else tried it as a one off, it would be considered rude and selfish.

Raven thought this behavioural acceptance was very cool and worth the investment over the years. She expected her mother-in-law to have a good cry, spill the beans and have a drinking session within the next few days. A husband going AWOL was a bit bigger than the usual interventions Raven managed. There might be a string of drinking sessions. Which was also a solid gold excuse to leave the management of the household and the kids to James. 'I'm going to get drunk with your mom James. Be home pretty late. Might stay over even. Love you all.' Raven had a good life.

However she was surprised. There was no crying. And only a partial and rather unsatisfactory bean spilling. At least the drinking started as soon as they were back at Wendy's house. Another thing just accepted about Raven. The daughter in law was invited home from the airport to spend some time with Wendy while the two sons with grandkids went home, after being taken for ice cream.

'You've travelled a good deal Raven. I've mainly travelled as part of mining company relocation processes in the last thirty years and travel has changed a lot.'

'Hitting the road old girl.'

'Yeah. I'm going to find Henry.'

'Who is…lost it would seem.'

'It's complicated.'

'And I am the daughter in law that doesn't ask questions. What do you need.'

'I need you to apologies for me.'

'For…?'

'Leaving.'

'Now.'

'Yes. I need to pack. And I was hoping you could help me with some tickets.'

'Sure. Miami. Las Vegas. The Big Apple. You're too old to carry the bags Wendy. James will be fine. What are we talking here? Six months in hiding with Henry.'

'Istanbul.'

'I can do Istanbul. Bucket list. The big bucket version.'

'I have to go on my own Raven. That's why I want someone to say goodbye for me. And it will be nice if it's you…'

'Well I appreciate…'

'…because you don't really care about people's feelings, so you won't mind doing it and you won't have to deal with people wanting to feel bad or confused about it because they'll know you're not interested.'

'Wow Wendy. Thanks…I think.'

'Book some tickets. I can wait around the subport for a while. I'll throw some things in my old backpack.'

'Wendy.' She looked back. 'Why Istanbul?'

'I heard some people talking on the ship. They'd heard the CEO say they were sending him there to be out of the way. Incognito. Said that it was the deal. No prosecution if Henry drops out of sight.'

Wendy was back in the living room more quickly than expected. Raven had booked flights that meant there would not be long to wait.

She got up and held her mother-in-law by the shoulders. 'Tickets booked, taxi coming, and unsatisfactory apologies composed. And…' Raven was not known for getting misty eyed.

Even when she was supposed to do so when something touching happened relating to the children. It was Raven. So it was okay. And yet here she was, getting misty eyed. Being Raven, she was allowed to do this if it suited her. '…and daughter in law commencing process of missing very important person in daughter in law's life.'

'We should have dropped that stupid 'in law' thing years ago.' Wendy smiled. 'And Raven.' She took the younger woman by the hands. 'If you know something's important. Someone's really important. Look past the small things to the big things. And don't hesitate.'

Raven smiled. 'Important advice. Keep in touch. Or not. Be careful. Or not. But come home. Not negotiable.'

'I'll be back. Hopefully not on my own. I love you. Favourite child.' They heard the cab's horn. 'And I'll deny I ever said that.'

Raven gave a lopsided smile. 'Forgotten already.'

Five hundred Elders, and a few thousand Malagan viewing on the screen the earthlings set up experienced something incredible.

Every other Malagan on the planet, wherever they were, and whatever they were doing, heard a Voice in their heads. The Voice was clear and spoke with authority. It was Semaj as she and her sister lay their hands upon the stone which was set deep in the ground.

'The day has come. My sister and I searched and waited all our lives for a Guide. Our Mother could bring us to life, but she, as was the case with our forebearers, could not bury knowledge in our minds…only our hearts. We needed an exceptional Malagan to nurture us, and a guide who knew her. Who would go where others would not, find what others would not find. And take us there. It was a human not a Malagan. A human who loves her. More than his life. And we found him.'

'We went there and saw what we were guided to see, and we communed with her. She is heartbroken that her gift of sentience has become less than she hoped. Mighty as she is, she cannot reignite what had grown up since her firstborn navigated her beauty, danger and bounty.'

'Her Envoys send her children this message.' Semaj's voice took on a tone and amplification not her own.'

'You can choose.'

The message continued. Eilrahc took over. Her nature now the appropriate messenger.

'Those who choose can live as you have these long millennia. Respected for your many strengths. And unchanged in the places you inhabit. Those who stay according to their free will shall always be respected and honoured for preserving the Malagan so long.'

'Other have choices. You might return to the ways of the original Stoics. Whose thoughts and way of life will be shared as they so scrupulously detailed them in books kept hidden. Indeed some may wish to blend their communities.'

'Or you can return to the beautiful towns and cities of the forests and plains. Recolonise them and tame their bounty only within their boundaries. Loving how they have preserved the varieties of fruits, grains, flowers, nuts and all manner of other gift for you to enjoy. Not sacred. But precious and treasured. You may create new places with friends or the like-minded.'

'Human's will never go into the bountiful lands. They take things precious to them and she is generous. They can take what they please from there. She admires the mercy they showed to the Malagan and that they left her people in peace. It might have been otherwise'.

Semaj resumed the narrative. 'Choices have their dangers. The risk of harm and sorrow come with new directions. Including the failure of communities. And now an opportunity unimagined. To go to earth. To visit. To live. And there your choice comes with many risks. Humans have virtues. Many capabilities and creativities and modes of living. However they can be cruel beyond our imaginings. Some abuse the vulnerable, hate what they fear, lie, cheat, steal, go to war and kill. Not by the thousands. By the millions. Their technologies, foods and creativity such as music are amazing to us. However some things can leave you addicted so you can do little else. Your visits and settlement would be carefully managed to limit such outcomes. This is not a choice.'

Her voice became her own. 'My beloved sister and I have a new mission now. We will be the bridge to Choices, and we will visit each Malagan community and speak to any who would like to meet with us. You cannot make a new choice without our approval, including recolonising the bountiful lands. Like it or not, we are the gatekeepers until all choices are made. We will provide some descriptions of the simplest of choices and if you can align yourself into a new community of the like-minded a change may not take long.

For those ready, confident and with a group large enough to succeed, we will meet with you the soonest, possibly help you engage with the Malagan from other communities so that the fulfilment of your choices can be swift. And the Struck outcasts will be given the same choices and any that wish to welcome them can let it be known. They are as much her children as any other.'

Eilrahc spoke. 'The Bekou and Botlu have preserved your choices for this day and should be afforded respect at all times for that. You come from a community of peace, whatever it's strictures, that you, in your choices, will be challenged to emulate while enjoying greater freedom. Those who remain to live as they have for millennia will always live in safety and have as much or as little interaction as they choose with those beyond their walls. Their communities, which sustained the Malagan for so long, will forever be the object of gratitude.'

'Now make quiet you minds. You are the Malagan. Long lived. Creativity, wisdom, affection and love are all yours to find and release from within to grow gradually and blossom.'

The two sisters were spent. They left the stage and fell into their mother arms and cried. The relief of a lifelong burden was lifted. And now another beckoned.

This second not so welcome given their nature. They, in a fashion, were to become a type of Bekou.'

They heard the Bekou speaking from the stage. The Botlu of Elders spoke from where they sat. The meeting ended and the marquee emptied. The Botlu calling the younger Malagan of their communities to them. The youth feared their Bekou would try to diminish the message or sway them to stay in their condition. However all accepted that the two were messengers representing unmatched authority, stripped of ritual.

Semaj and Eilrahc sat peacefully. Each holding a hand of their mother and the other with their sister. Their mother felt a tranquillity. Unimaginable. Only Henry had ever experience it.

They saw the Bekou standing at a distance. As if waiting for them to notice her. They called her over. The old Malagan was surprised that she was welcomed by all three. Tensions forgotten. Everyone could stay as they had been all these long years. They had only given those that wanted a choice to do so. 'I consulted with the Botlu. They asked me to tell you that all are ready to assist you. She that gave you the message is our life.'

The two walked over and give the old Malagan the first embrace she had ever known. It was very strange and beautiful. And like Henry, she was filled with a kind of joy, foreign even to humans, who were accustomed to feeling so much more. There were very few others who would share that experience with the two Envoys as they were now known. It was their way of showing their appreciation that, disagree as they might have done, the old Bekou had worked for balance, wherever it could be found, in a community in which balance was scarce.

Henry wanted her to have a journey. She knew that. So she made time for it. She visited beautiful places, ate amazing food, met interesting people, saw beautiful things. And always asked around as she searched the city and then the countryside. She was in a little town where they made some of the most beautiful pottery in Turkey. A place renowned for it. A man she met had insisted she go to a particular establishment some distance out of Istanbul because it was the best. The owner took her into a little room and with the lights out the beautiful vases, bowls and dishes glowed with an eerie phosphorescence.

She told him it was magnificent, but she couldn't afford anything and she was travelling.

He'd heard this a hundred times. He smiled. 'Whenever I hear this I say that the main pleasure in my life is to show off the incredible skill of our Turkish craftsman. There are those that can afford it, and they allow all to enjoy it.'

She was smiling. She was relaxed with people almost always now. It was the first time she'd travelled alone, and she found it liberating. She loved being a daughter, wife, mother, grandmother and friend. She also realised she loved this life, and it was okay. She had nothing to worry about and had only one question in her life. 'Have you seen him'. She had a photo and told people who he was. It was the story more than the photo that ignited an interested in the man. Many had been Henry. Experienced things just as he had and found it life changing. They were full of their own questions, but none had seen him. Except for this man. 'He couldn't fool me. My daughters had insisted I watch…or experience the immersion. I have never engaged with such things. I became somewhat fascinated which I believe is not uncommon.' The man laughed. 'His disguise when he was passing through here…ha…when I revealed I recognised him without difficulty he was a little embarrassed. Though it must have worked well enough on others.'

'Did he tell you anything.'

'He would not discuss his time on Malagan. We talked about our lives. He spoke of his adventures in Turkey. He spoke fondly of his family. I assume he communicates with them in the life of anonymity he endeavours to create.'

'He lives in Turkey still? Do you think. I'm not, a journalist or some…weird stalker.'

The man laughed. 'I know who you are. He spoke fondly of you in particular. No he left Turkey. Said he was going to…somewhere in Asia I think.'

Shit. Thought Wendy. Asia's a pretty big place.

He smiled knowingly and went to see if his wife remembered. He came back a while later. 'She wasn't sure initially. However after we consulted a map we were both certain. A place called Bali. In…Indonesia. Sounds exotic.'

Wendy tended to frame things in a pleasant way much more now. 'I'm certain Turkey is at least as exotic to the Balinese.'

He felt uncomfortable deceiving her. He made what he hoped were some nice embellishments. The men who had been there told him the simple truth. Henry, after his experiences on Malagan, believed his wife needed an adventure.

And time to reflect as to whether she wanted to be with him. They worded their message carefully such that it might be construed that Henry was actually in Bali.

The man told them he would think on it and that they should come again the next day. The person he married, whose advice he followed scrupulously in business and personal matters thought for some time. 'The man in the immersion recording left that planet wiser. Whatever else people may say of him, nearly all agree on that. And from my observation he was already a good man before he had his adventure. He believes this is good for his wife. What would you say?'

'Deception in this rare case might be considered a good thing?' It would be an anathema for them to lie in any normal dealings in their lives.

'Those two Malagan...trusted Henry. And look at the changes which have been brought to the lives of millions. We should trust his judgement. And yours my love. And think on the fact that these people sought you out because you are known to be an honourable man. Ultimately you must be at peace you can do this without dishonour.'

•• ———————— ••●•• ———————— ••

Not many people came into Lester's office and were offered a scotch. Especially not the kind in Lester's cabinet. However this visitor was doing something interesting. And important.

'So how goes your little project.'

'Henry stayed a little longer than planned and left Lithuania after just under a year and has taken his language and pizza making skills to cattle ranch a few hundred miles out of Buenos Aires.'

'Lithuanian and pizza making being a prerequisite for that kind of work I'm sure.'

'As requested, we offered some help. He's held up his side of the deal. He said he was happy with what he had. Which is close to nothing from what I could tell.'

'Way too spiritual for me.'

'I preferred the four stars the company so generously supplied me with.'

'And his pilgrim. Come to her senses and gone home.'

'No. Bumped into a chap in Bali though. They bumped into each other pretty hard it appears. On a few occasions. Short but sweet. So say the staff at the hotel they worked together in.

She's traipsing around the wilds of Scotland as we speak.'

'You know; I wanted to bury him deep for the rest of his life. But there's a transience to everything these days. He wanted an outcome, so he didn't have to pay for his sins in jail, and I didn't want to put him there and have people hate the Company, and me, for doing it. At the time I didn't think I could let him get away with it. Now…it doesn't really matter. Maybe let him know that. When you see him next.'

'Which would be never unless you want to send me four star to Buenos Aires.' Lester wasn't well known for wasting a dime. 'Send him a phone. I imagine he doesn't have one. Line up a video call. Maybe he'll let his wife rest her weary…bones.'

'In a few months, if she believes the artfully contrived 'Henry' sightings we've embedded and the tenuous evidence of his whereabouts, she'll be off to a place called Tasmania. I had to look that one up. After which the breadcrumb trail ends and she's on her own.'

Lester laughed. 'Going to Tasmania to somehow figure out her husband is, what do they call it…poking cows…in South America.'

'You know boss. I've met Henry twice and never met his wife in person and yet it's like I know them. And I think those star-crossed lovers will meet again. What happens then is anybody's guess.'

'Thanks for the way you've managed this. I'd like you to keep a close eye on both of them. If either of them gets in some real trouble, we call in the local cavalry to pull them out.'

'A pleasure boss.'

Wendy sat with Raven. 'It's been over two years. I thought it would be a few months.'

The favourite child was with someone uncertain about what to do. Wendy had been home a month. She'd run out of leads in Tasmania, which turned out to be a beautiful place with friendly people. But no one had seen Henry. There were other sensations that had come and gone in the world, and the pictures she had were a few years old even before she'd left.

Raven was confident. 'There's nothing else for it Wendy. Pack that bag. This time I'm coming. Three more years. Five tops. We'll find him. Drilling ice core in Antarctica maybe. Though we might look there last.'

Wendy started crying. 'I can't find him. The world's too big and I need a rest from travelling.' She knew she didn't want to stop travel altogether though. 'I loved it. I am so grateful for what Henry…ha…put me through. But I've given up believing I can find him. And anyway, if he finds me he probably won't…'

She started crying in earnest.

'Oh. Full scale adventure was it.'

'It…I was on the verge of giving up or maybe the journey had become more about me than Henry. Which I know is what he wanted. And then…' She sighed. 'One thing led to another. It wasn't…long-lasting. But it was sweet. Beautiful even.'

'Wendy, I think Henry came away from that place with some smarts. Maybe he wanted you to know…experience what he did. Sweet and beautiful. In a different way maybe. I don't think he'll really care now.' She breathed in deeply and gave out the big Raven huff of having made a decision. Usually someone had to look out when that happened. She had accepted it should be subtle and let the star crossed lovers think it had happened by fate. 'I think we should celebrate this breakthrough with a family dinner at O'Grady's.'

'Raven I'm not so keen on the family…celebrating this specific break through.'

'Family dinner. Hold the celebration.'

'I guess so but could go somewhere else this time. We had the welcome home dinner there and the menu is…not that great these days.' She now had the food appreciation perspective of a globe trotter.

'Trust in the good judgement of your almost magical daughter.'

A man had piqued Raven's curiosity during the welcome home dinner when she was going to the restroom and he had come out to go the men's room in the restaurant as the staff restrooms were out of order. He had turned away to go the other way back into the kitchen. There had been a flicker of recognition. She tracked him down and watched him. When she confronted him he said he'd heard Wendy was coming back, via Lester's man in this case, and he'd come home and got some work. He said once she'd 'settled in' they might…cross paths.

The family were a little bemused to be having another dinner at the same place they'd eaten a few weeks before. People didn't argue with Raven unless they had a very good reason.

And experience told them that it would be Raven who adjudicated whether they had a good reason or not. It was usually not.

It had been a nice meal. Raven advised them they were all having desert. 'Or the cheese board if you have to. Come with me Wendy.' They disappeared into the kitchen.

The two chefs had been warned to expect visitors to walk into the kitchen and they were to leave them both 'the hell alone'.'

'Hey Man Bun, this has gone on long enough. Your good lady wife is worn out from looking for you.'

The man had been assiduously scrubbing a pot. The chefs appreciated how clean he got them though they sometimes struggled to understand his thick Lithuanian accent. A man looked up. He had a ginger beard and a sleeve of tattoo's along one arm and another on his back as the branches of a strange tree running up from behind his shirt to his hairline on the back of his neck. There were round wire rim glasses and most egregious of all was the tightly pulled back hair terminating in a man bun.

For a moment Wendy thought maybe Raven was taking her to someone with yet another clue.

When he looked up and smiled the disguise, which was rather good, vanished around familiar features. She didn't wait thirty seconds. She had decided that long before. He didn't need to wait to see if she loved him. So they met in the middle. And said nothing for a long time.

'Was the journey worth it.'

She smiled. 'It was worth it. Thankyou. I have so many memories. I treasure them. They're mine. I understand now.' Wendy believed that, even though it would spoil the moment, she had to let Henry know at the outset. If she waited, and if it mattered to him, it would be as if she'd told him once was too late. 'I have to tell you something before…'

'Raven told me about that. Don't' worry. It was part of the Journey. It's like me. I have something I'll never tell anyone about. It's too special.'

'I've watched the whole movie a few times, with Raven, and listened to all the commentary about those missing hours.' She smiled. 'I think your secret is different to mine.'

'It's still secret and special. Unforgettable and something I don't want to, don't need to and will never speak of.'

Wendy was relieved. 'Quite a look you've got happening there. Is that going to be the new Henry.'

He laughed and pulled off the bun and thew it at one of the chefs. It fell in some soup. 'Arturas. What the...' He fished it out. 'This travesty was fake all along. Do you have any idea how many people I told we had this weird guy working for us with a man bun.'

Next Henry carefully pulled off a fake ginger beard which had a grey patch in the middle. 'The tattoos on my arm are only the ink without the needle. I get new ones every now and then. Except the tree at the back.'

'Henry...?' The chef was making connections. The locals were aware the Henry was from their town. But he'd disappeared after his adventure. And he'd hardly been seen around much even before he left the planet.

'Could we stick with Arturas. And can I keep my job. I like working with you guys.'

'Sure. No man bun though. And I'm not sure you'll get away with the ordinary life thing.'

'It'll be a flash in the pan like everything these days. I'll only need to let people know how boring I am.' To Wendy and Raven he said. 'Let's go and see the kids.'

A few weeks later Wendy let Henry know that 'the young ladies' were going to be interviewed on a tonight show. He thanked her and said he was going to be busy with his woodwork. A craft he'd pretended to take up. Wendy assumed it was so he could keep dancing in secret because very little woodwork got done. However Henry did what he'd been doing for years now. He'd stand in the room and hold up his arms and recapture it. Even with two missing pieces it was indescribable.

The show was in the top ten ratings worldwide. In history. The two had spoken with many earthlings as individuals and thousands of Malagan. But never done an interview. Yet so many humans and Malagan had been them or had been Henry and shared what was a beautiful, fascinating and innocent adventure. Respected, loved, desired and occasionally lusted after though less than might have been expected. Even when they had played at being seductive it hadn't been in the least erotic. Somehow though, no one could experience the journey and not come away...better. When not managing the choices of the Malagan, they spent a great deal of time travelling over the wildest and most remote places on earth. Bare foot. None knew that this was not because they wanted to.

All the choices for those who wanted to try something different had been made on Malagan. Some had even moved to live with those who had been outcasts; the Stuck who were invited everywhere, even to the communities that chose no other changes.

Their main occupation was with the organisations they collaborated with to facilitate the Malagan who chose to spend time on earth. Initially in small communities of their own kind to acclimatise to the 'short days' and the climate of where they wanted to visit. Then with families like those that might host an exchange student. And then a transition into a new life. The latter was a slow process and required a great deal of time in managed environments before a staged migration into full integration into earth society. Even then it was like being on parole. Few had made it to unfettered habitation on earth, as Semaj and Eilrahc felt accountable for each of them and worked closely with the authorities, organisations and families. In the interview they described this process in detail.

The day would come when what they had created would sustain itself. And they would hand over the process on both planets. That day was still far in the distance though.

Most of the interview, by prior agreement, was about the progress of having some Malagan come to stay on earth.

In spite of some early fears that earth would be swamped by aliens, it was clear to all now that numbers would always be small and only a fraction would choose to settle, though almost none would regret the visit. They had agreed to allow the host of the show to ask a few other questions without notice. 'What really happened in those hours missing from the immersion recording.' It was inevitable. Eilrahc made the answer they had responded with so many times when asked. To Malagan or human.

'Something innocent, beautiful and private. They were the best of moments. Incomparable. We know Henry feels the same.'

'And do you see Henry.'

'No. I think our friendship is more delightful to us as a memory. We have travelled widely and found none better. Although you have a great many good people here on earth.'

'You've travelled to more places on earth than anyone I've ever heard of. Yet you don't visit cities and towns very much.'

The two looked at each other. 'We are messengers.' The said in unison.

The interviewer experienced a powerful desire, a compulsion almost, to ask no more questions. They thanked him for his interest and left to the music they had been arrested by. 'I'd go the whole wide world just to find her.' It was especially true for them now.

Years passed. Henry grew old. He had never revisited the full immersion recording Carlos had captured, who was one of the few he maintained a close contact with. Henry never enquired about the 'girls'.' He loved 'woodwork' and his family. Visitors and family members had learned he wasn't interested in the news of the world. He read books and poems that were, in some cases, hundreds of years old.

In his early nineties, he was suddenly bedridden and found it difficult to speak. Doctors gave him six months with a diagnosis of a strange tumour that had appeared without warning. Wendy only just ninety, had had a rich life spending time with Henry and without him. On journeys in some cases lasting years. One with Raven. Or doing volunteer work abroad and a few times helping with the process of integrating Malagan. Living as a sort of house mother in their first stop transition communities.

Henry slept much of the day away and when awake seemed to have a peaceful mind with nothing much going on in it.

One day he looked up to see Semaj and Eilrahc at his bedside. Not touched in the slightest by age but for their eyes and a slight tempering to their tendency to mischief. 'He would flee this life sister. Without a word of farewell to those whom he fooled into believing were worthy of his friendship.'

'So poor our fellowship must have been.'

'A true man. Yet strategically hurtful our Henry. A paradox.'

Henry beamed. He couldn't speak much now but he didn't need or want to. He didn't make any indication he might want to take their hand or sit up in an awkward embrace. They one as lay there, and he again felt an agelessness and beauty of another world but also now melded with his world. He knew they had something to share, and they waited a little longer until Wendy joined them as they had orchestrated the timing such that her arrival would come soon after theirs. She walked in. With a cane now having worn out her knees, she looked around her and was astonished to see the pair who had had such a remarkable effect of their lives.

They looked young but felt old. And like her she got a sense that they were now tired of the whole adventure. Exciting and fascinating as it had been. However they carried a sadness she could not fathom. Smiling Eilrahc said. 'How grateful we are that Henry could share a life with one who would go so far, indeed to an unreasonable extent, to demonstrate her love for him.'

'It was a wonderful journey, and it helped me to understand, at least a little.'

They came across and each took her by the hand. She understood what they were asking and didn't need words. They helped her to a chair. She sat quietly and then nodded.

Semaj wanted to say it though. 'She has called him home.'

Wendy also now understood why their loss, in a way, would be greater than hers. 'I'll return tomorrow so that his family have had time to bid him farewell.' Said Semaj.

Raven took on the role of managing the comings and goings of relatives giving a farewell to Henry. Carlos flew overnight from Spain dropping everything the moment Raven called him. Grandchildren arrived some with great grandchildren. Most stayed briefly because Henry couldn't reply. However a few, like Carlos and Raven, sat and reminisced.

Wendy shared the almost complete details of the journey she took to find him, which she she'd never done. Because Raven had control of the schedule, she was there when Semaj arrived at the door.

She had the same experience so many had when they encountered an Envoy. Indescribable. And a sense of understanding it all at last. However, for the first time ever Semaj and Eilrahc were not together. Semaj would manage what was going to happen, but she felt a kind of emptiness she had never dreamed would exist within her.

Raven was who she was because of a rapid and subtle insightfulness about the complexities people. She could then deliver an observation or decision with confidence. Then the requisite action or inaction occured in its wake. She knew the pair had been inseparable since childhood because their whole life story had eventually been revealed.

'I've never loved someone...like that.' She said to Semaj. 'I can't imagine it.'

Semaj nodded and asked the woman with such a young mind, in a body in its sixties. 'Will you come?'

Raven smiled and said. 'Hell yeah.'

Henry slept for most of the Hotshot the Company was only too pleased to provide. Exciting as it was for Raven, who had never been off world, let alone with an Envoy, it was quickly apparent that there would be not much in the way of conversation from Semaj. The Envoy was a little embarrassed by this. Raven's native wisdom blended with confidence tended to fix such things. 'I love to read. I hope you don't mind.' And the other relaxed and knew they could travel in peace. Raven was convivial, as was her nature, with the crew and the few passengers in the main cabin.

She awoke halfway through what was the ships night cycle, calibrating a little each night to the destination. She found Henry was being moved via a hatch at the Malagan spaceport to a small medical craft with a bay to house a few beds such as the one he was in. There was only a pilot and Semaj. Raven knew this was the time assigned for her to farewell Henry. However Semaj, in another unfamiliar experience; vacillated. 'Come a little further if you would.'

The craft landed in a small dell with a low cliff embracing it in perhaps two hundred and seventy degrees of rock arms. The opening looked out on a beautiful land. Raven realised it was so much more beautiful even than people in a 'immersion' could appreciate.

'Bid farewell to the one who loved you as a daughter. This is his most beloved place. And mine…and my sister's.' Raven took Henry by the hand, and he left the bed for the first time in months. He was able to hold Raven in his arms for a long time. And whisper. 'Favourite child'.

She took the bed with her as she went. Uncertain as to what was to befall Henry. There was no grave ready to receive him.

When she had gone, he looked around. Concerned. 'Eilrahc?'

'She abides on earth now Henry. It's a strange tale. Improbable. Again you were the troublemaker. Walking around barefoot here and on earth. You brought some of earth here with you. And took some Malagan on your return. Of course there was a deep fascination. To fly endlessly through space and then find you are not alone. After uncountable aeons believing it was so. My sister and I became…love letters. Visiting all the remote corners on both the worlds. Marvelling at the wonders. Ha. However Henry, one tires even of wonders for the purpose of sharing the essence of the two most unlikely of lovers.' This solicited a wan smile.

'However they could never truly commune. And paid the price of incautious infatuation. They have resolved to return to their former ways. To love and nurture and forgive that which clothes them. However…they decided a gift from each, as a remembrance…a sweet memory. A keepsake.' Semaj was silent for a long time. Tears were beginning to trickle down her cheeks. The Malagan did not cry. 'We wandered far. We found the earth's biggest living being was a vast connected colony of beautiful trees. And there she abides. Part of huge, connected life, that might be razed to the ground only to be reborn.' The tears now landed on the soft turf where they stood barefoot. 'I brought something of her to be with us.' She drew from her pocket, a small swathe of the fine auburn hair her sister had. Tears now falling on it. 'However I realise now…I cannot hold it in my hand.'

Henry smiled. That sweet, generous, loving smile all who knew him appreciated. He knelt down and pulled up some of the soft turf opening a small divot of soil. 'It was here?' He could say a little. She nodded. Where she had stood on that perfect day. She placed the lock in the small hole and covered it over with the soil and grass.

She looked up to smile at Henry.

Now with sweet sorrow rather than grief. She was one ripe, ready, at peace and grateful. She led him to the place to stand and she went to hers. 'Raise up your hands Henry.' He closed his eyes. His mind was all at once as clear and fresh and as free as it had ever been. He knew his fingers were making tiny motions as if leaves caught by a slight breeze. This time he felt his feet changing, disappearing into the soft turf and beyond. His mind came to join his friend's, and he wrapped his around her with comfort and solace. His legs formed a solid trunk. His skin grew tough, and his mind drifted into a vast, slow place. A small piece of his consciousness abiding there. Within a phenomenal whole.

Lem had brought her child here every few weeks since she had returned to Malagan a year before. No one else ever came, well known as it was yet she alone felt drawn to the place and welcome where others felt a reverence and were never inclined to visit. She had been on a program to settle on earth and had met a Malagan who'd been there for years and was only now on occasional 'parole' visits. He had decided to gender identify, which was optional and so had adopted the dress and bearing of a male. She had decided to take the feminine approach.

This gender outweighed the male and neutrals partly because Eilrahc and Semaj and been such an inspiration to so many. The sisters had accepted the thousands upon thousands of Malagan's aspirants with their prodigious minds and helped them on a journey. And were tender, but firm, when the choice, the Malagan had been free to make initially, was deemed to be a bad one. Many Malagan had begun to appreciate humour and there was a common refrain. 'We are free to choose, until the Envoys unchoose for us.'

Lem and her mate had a child. However after a year she decided earth was too noisy, fast and in some places dirty and dangerous. Her partner wanted to travel and work in a variety of occupations some at which the Malagan excelled because they were patient and gentle while being quick witted, intelligent and scholarly. As with the Malagan everywhere, individual points of view gradually coalesced. Once mature there came a consensus. The two separated. With a brief expression of affection, only because they had learned the behaviour from the humans. They had developed emotions, yet were forgetful of them quickly, as they retreated to the mindset of their old community if that best suited their situation.

Lem had moved to the original city visited by the trio. It was popular for that reason and a vibrant place. There were other original towns and cities, and new towns were being established throughout Malagan. But none closer to the dell she was drawn to. As with Henry, Lem loved it so, and loved the feeling the place gave her and the strange nurturing her child received from going there.

There were two old trees positioned as if looking out over the vista. And between them a beautiful young tree that she had never seen anywhere else on Malagan. It had a white bark and lost its leaves each year. She'd lean back on one of the trees as her child played on the grass or climbed over rocks or sat in the trees branches when she would lift him there. They'd have a beautiful meal of the fruits and nuts brought from her garden and the gardens of friends. As it grew dark, her child, exhausted, and by the light of some glowing sconces, would curl in her lap and sleep and so would she. Both would dream of music. And dancing.

Intersection

'Hit me.'

This was how John sometimes started his appointments. Some patients liked a question-and-answer approach. So that's what he did. But some preferred to get everything out in a disorganised mess. They would then pick through what was important, or even maybe the interesting. The session might be spent on what was disclosed or either of them might suggest another topic to investigate. Patients from the more difficult backgrounds frequently engaged well with John because being random was sometimes a better reflection of how they lived, and how they thought. It worked better for him than trying to impose some discipline on a session. His colleagues did not always support the approach however he'd had good results, until more recent times.

Sunny had come from an unimaginably traumatic childhood setting and had been on the streets since she was eleven.

After being arrested for several petty crimes, she was put in a diversion program and, relative to where she started, she was now in a much better place. She was settled in a managed share house, had a job and a circle of friends that didn't do drugs. She was faithfully making the meetings with the Program officer she was assigned to and was hoping to move out and share a house with some friends when her time was up.

But today she was anxious and wondering how she was going to get through without a cigarette. After John said. 'Hit me.' There was silence.

'Pretty bad huh.' John usually made an effort to listen carefully to his patients and restrain his natural urge to make things a conversation, or, contrary to the intent of the sessions, give specific advice. For patients like Sunny, when she was like this, if he only wanted to listen there would be long awkward silences because some things she had always simply refused to talk about.

She was whispering, which he hadn't heard in six months. 'Lost my job. Got into a real bad fight with Jess. I'm angry all the time now. The thoughts. They've started coming back the way they used to.'

'Let's deal with one thing at a time. That job simply wasn't working.' This was an example of what John was not supposed to do. However he believed he was on solid ground from what he'd heard. 'Do we need to go through why?' John had heard enough to know that Sunny's situation and outlook were completely at odds with the woman she worked for, and he didn't know how much was going to be gained by delving into it. 'You tried hard? Did the best you could?'

She looked up as if she had to explain herself. 'I really tried but she…'

'Forget it Sunny. It's done. That's something you think you're supposed feel bad about so that's what you're doing. The real thing… is you feel bad about what happened with Jess. Was it a fifty-fifty thing or…you know, you lost your job, you're feeling angry, fighting with the painful thoughts. Seventy thirty; because it's tough at the moment.'

'Ninety to ten I reckon.'

'You sorry?'

'Yeah. I said a lot of things. She's always been good to me…like mostly. Never uses me up like some so-called friends do.'

'So call her. Simple message. I was a bitch. Said a bunch of things I regret. I'm sorry. I understand if you don't want to be my friend anymore. That's about all I can do about this Jess. You can't change how Jess reacts; you can only do the best you can. It's hard to say you're sorry, even when you're wrong. But in situations like this it takes a load off immediately, however she responds. And her response might change once things sink in. She might not say it's all cool straight away. So call her.'

'Now.'

'Never wait to make things as right as they can be. I'll get a coffee. You?' She nodded. Another thing he wasn't supposed to do. He broke rules and was willing to accept the consequences if there were any. It turned out there were consequences. He also knew the advice to make things right as soon as possible was complete hypocrisy in his own personal life.

When he came back, she said. 'She swore at me for a while. I had to tell her I was wrong a couple of times for her to know I meant it. She said she was…glad we got it sorted.'

'While you were on the call I talked to a guy. He's a Parole Officer but that can mean he has some good contacts for jobs and other services the program doesn't plug you into. He said he's going to make some calls and if he turns anything up, we'll have a three-way conference call about it.'

'I always come away from here with some of my problems fixed John. No other place is like that. I gotta fill out ten forms to get told I was never eligible in the first place.'

This was the part of John's job he liked the best. 'Money coming in that you've earned. Decent roof over your head and living with people that care about you. These are the things that give people dignity, a feeling they're in control of their lives and a sense of security. If you took everyone on the streets and got them those three things, I think only a third or so would go back. You need to remember you can get and keep a hold of them Sunny. Even if you have a bad setback.'

Irrespective of that, her life was still being impacted by her traumatic memories and dark anger that was sometime barely below the surface. She wanted to talk about something she'd heard might make a big difference. 'This religious guy visits the house sometimes, I'm not sure which type he fronts for. Nice bloke. He says if I can just learn to forgive people, these dark feeling could go away.'

'You tried it?'

'No.' She said quietly.

'I have this theory about forgiveness. Or it grew out of something I read in a surprisingly poorly edited novel. Our society couldn't function without forgiveness. Lots of little things. I bump into someone and the spill their coffee. I say, hey sorry about that do you want a fresh one. I have a fight with my friend, and I was wrong. I call her and say I was wrong. Sorry. I cut someone off on the road and they give me a blast on the horn. When they pass, I give them a wave saying sorry. They've done the same to somebody else. People might stay angry after an incident out on the road. That's their problem. Our society usually accepts an apology. But only up to…' He shrugged. '…and imprecise level of wrong doing. Things that are forgotten by the next day or even it might take a month. Little stuff gets forgiven or forgotten. Except by…hah…dumb people or those unlucky enough to have a very unforgiving frame of mind. Then there's some religions or philosophies that say forgiveness is both a cure all and in some cases a requirement.'

'But…Sunny…someone kills my baby? No. I'm never going to forgive them. Why would I. Someone abuses a vulnerable girl, am I going to forgive them. No way. There are spiritual people who have their approaches, and it may work for them. I know it wouldn't work for me. But I don't know everything. Far from it. If there's a chance it might work for you, give it a shot. But remember if people do very bad things and simply get forgiven, what have they learned. How will they react the next time if society or an individual has been permissive the first time around? Usually, even in the religious context, the forgiveness happens when people genuinely repent and are sometimes still punished. And maybe that is a set up you could agree with. Maybe you're inclined to forgive. But I think you should do that if you believe it's right for you, not because it's the recommendation of a guy who possibly hasn't had to forgive anyone for something horrendous. Because he's never experienced anything like that.'

'I can't imagine…' She stared into space. She had started to secretly think there was something wrong with her. Because she couldn't forgive.

With a specific sub set of Clients John had fallen into the habit of advice giving which he would not normally agree with. However sometimes Sunny didn't wanted to talk too much but she did want a conversation. 'Sunny sometimes people hear of a virtue and think, or are told, it can be applied universally. We're told humility and not being aggressive are virtues. But to a workplace psychopath, humble or passive people are exactly what they want. So they can manipulate them. Hurt them with no consequences.'

'Deep down I think I'd be lying to myself.'

'I've suggested it won't work but I should encourage you to try things, however only with you in the driver's seat. You might come back and teach me a thing or two. If something works, I don't care where it comes from. But never surrender that driver's seat Sunny. That's advice outside of my professional boundaries. And I think you know when I'm doing that. I feel strongly about it though. Because there are a lot of people in the world who'd like to take over that driver's seat. Or sit next to you and become a navigator.' He laughed. 'I'm in danger of being in the second category though aren't I.'

'Yeah but that's okay Doctor John. I know you're not wanting to keep sitting there doing that.'

His tone become more serious. Sunny didn't like talking about what happened to her.

She would talk about where it had left her, but she would become intensely emotional and anxious if she tried to revisit the details in therapy. 'For now, let's talk about the dark thoughts. The bad news is they might always be there. The good news is they can gradually become much less powerful, more of an occasional experience. They may affect your mood, but nowhere near as dramatically as they do now. But imagine if those thoughts have an important purpose? Think about whether there is a reason, and believe it or not, a good reason why you have them. They are way out of whack in terms of intensity and frequency Sunny. But then again, they're in response to some really serious shit. So don't think there's something wrong with you for having them. They're telling you, urgently, what to keep away from. Reminding you of terrible danger. But there's a problem. And guess what. It's not with you. In healthy societies people who have had those terrible experiences are drawn into a safe and nurturing environment and this takes over an important space in the mind where those thoughts were. One reason you ended up on the streets is you had no nurturing or safe place to go. So your mind had empty spaces to fill. And it's going to sometimes fill up those empty spaces with the only thing it's known. And they are powerful and dramatic.

Awful memories and emotions and things the mind is very naturally going to feel fear and anxiety about. So that's a big part of why they come back, they find a space to fill.'

She sat digesting this. Eyes downcast.

'Have you ever tried mediating?'

'I know you told me to. And I…'

'Ha…didn't have much success.' He laughed. 'I'm lousy at it but if you want to understand what I'm saying, try meditating. Not because you need to start it as a practice, although there's plenty of evidence that it's good for your mind. But Sunny initially it puts into stark relief what I'm talking about. You empty your mind and realise how hard it is to maintain that state. Nature doesn't usually like a vacuum. Things will immediately get into the empty spaces you've made, even if they are banal and boring thoughts. Unlike many people, you have some very unpleasant things which can fill the spaces. Ironically, this is to remind you not to put yourself at risk of those things happening. As if you need to be told. Ha. Minds can be pretty dumb.'

'I wish I could tell my mind I figured that shit out already.'

He laughed. 'I spend most of my day with people wishing their God damn mind would give them a break and do as it's told. One way to give it the message is do what you're doing. Try to surround you with good things to look at, healthy, normal experience and think about. And gradually reduce the negative thoughts and feelings so that they become a part, believe it or not, part of your healthy mind. These were your early years. Rather than try to blot them out, though you try hard not to dwell on them, you set them in a context of healthy thoughts and the good lifestyle you've worked hard to achieve. Even if there are occasional setbacks. Maybe serious setbacks. People like Jess are an example of the fact there are good people who stick by you as a friend even if you've been a bit bitchy.'

He spoke to her more seriously. As if they were both professionals. 'I've been reminded by those who review my consultation notes that some clinicians want me to go back and revisit what happened in detail with patients. I don't do that, and the literature is divided. But think about it in case it's what you'd like to try.' John usually had two phones on his desk. On this occasion there was only one. He'd had to use his work phone which he didn't usually do for these kinds of arrangements. It started to vibrate. He looked up and pointed so she knew the call was about her.

After a brief exchange he finished the call and said. 'How about washing and detailing cars at a car yard? A bit above the award.'

She thought for only a moment. 'Yeah, I could do that.'

'Okay. My man is going to line up an interview. I've sent him your details.'

There was an awkward silence. He knew what it was about and only she could fill it. She was hesitant and a little anxious. 'This is the last appointment for the Program, and I know some of the things you've done aren't what the Program's supposed to do. I wanted to let you know how much it's meant to me.'

'There's no goodbyes from me Sunny, unless you want there to be one. It's a see you around if you don't need any help from me anymore. The day may come, pretty likely believe it or not, when I've fucked my life up so badly, I'll be coming to you for some help and advice.' She smiled at that. She also got a sense that as far as he was concerned it was not beyond the realms of possibility. 'I know the people in the Diversion Program well. We can keep having these meetings at the same frequency or whatever suits you Sunny.

You tell me the day and I'll get a meeting room in their offices lined up. They'll happen around lunch time. And I'm always a phone call away as you know.'

'Now you need to fill that head up with good things. Music in your headphones that doesn't make you feel bad. Page books, talking books, pod casts, movies, voluntary work, renovate furniture, write books or start drawing. See if you like a musical instrument or learn Mindfulness. Throw it all around and see what sticks. Don't expect miracles. Expect a return on your efforts along with the occasional kick in the guts life seems to make a condition of breathing.'

At the end of the session, which ran overtime, they stood and John said. 'Not allowed to give you a hug.' As he held her at a distance with hands on her shoulders he said. 'This is going to be a much better month for you Sunny. And if you have problems call me, text me whatever. It's the phone I keep for you and a couple of other people so if it rings, I answer it any time day or night. We can fix anything.' She smiled and left.

That night at home the same ineradicable tensions pervaded the space between himself and his wife Patrice. Their last remaining child at home, Hazel, was preparing for the school drama production the following night, which was a prestigious event in the school calendar.

Hazel had a middling role in the cast, which she was excited about because getting any role was an achievement. Patrice had made it abundantly clear she was sick of hearing about what he did during the day and running a business providing her services and a couple of people she had on the books as relief hairdressers didn't always provide much in the way of conversation topics. She talked about what the other children were up to, however John seemed to be someone who, once they had left the nest, wasn't as involved as he'd been when they were at home. A phase during which he often ended up being 'the good guy' without making much effort. Or perhaps it was because of his approach compared to the efforts Patrice. These were about things she either felt strongly about or obliged to comment on. Once they were out in the wide world, he apparently saw himself as mainly there if they wanted some advice, which happened only occasionally, but it was listened to because they'd asked for it. If they ignored it, they knew their old man wouldn't care. Maybe, Patrice thought, he didn't even care much if they'd listened.

This was close to the opposite of what she did. Consequently when they were home, John was relaxed with them and chatted about whatever they wanted to and maybe he would share some deidentified details of his work.

Sometimes with a message buried within that might be useful, but wrapped in an amusing anecdote. For her, the visits could be pleasant, but there was usually some underlying tension about one issue or another. And what was frustrating was she had very often taken an interest in things which had saved her children making significant mistakes, or helped them to realise an opportunity, or had helped them see some different perspectives. It was the density and delivery of advice and observations that they struggled with. Never her intentions.

Things had taken a turn for the worse in the last few weeks. This change was brought about because of a discovery Patrice had made. Her attitude had turned ice cold and now grew even colder when John failed to respond appropriately, or at all in fact, to the sudden drop in temperature.

Mid-morning the next day John was ahead of time so decided to get a takeaway coffee. He used to ask around the office if anyone wanted one, but as the practice had expanded, there was too many to order. He would get Beth one if she wanted it. It would be hard to imagine a person better suited to meeting people who were struggling with life and helping them with the administration aspects of interacting with a clinician.

She was good natured and friendly and very capable at managing appointments, invoices and referrals. If anyone was rude to her, she gave them cues to suggest it was a bad idea because she didn't really have to be helpful at all if she chose not to be. If there was any hint of violence or intimidation, four psychiatrists and five psychologists would unify, even if it was a patient in a difficult situation and kick them out, telling them they had one more chance. But not on that day. The manager of the Clinic, Tent Wickham, said many a time that the first duty of the clinic was the safety but also mental health of the people who worked there.

John was standing up to go to the cafe. Somehow the knock said it all but the eyes of the two men entering the room confirmed it. Trent and colleague.

After they told him John could only initially manage the cliché. 'No. No. That's bullshit. She left here yesterday in a good frame of mind. She was moving forward. Getting outside support. In control of her... life.' As he'd seen on some dramas, he swept everything off his desk. 'This is bullshit.'

'We're so sorry John.' Trent was empathetic, but in his voice, there was a real concern he'd brought news like this to John one too many times in the recent past.

John didn't regret his little burst of anger and looked at the desk devoid of files, stationary, family photos and the few objects he valued from his travels. One in particular from New Zealand. A Humpback whale carved from whale bone. He's smuggled it in. The fin was broken off by the outburst.

'How about I take you out for a coffee. It's warm and… there's a bit of sunshine for a change.' Trent nearly used the word Sunny. 'I'll see you in five.' He said this in case John wanted to put his desk back in order.

The man who'd come to support him stayed after Trent had left. 'Thanks for coming along Saj.' The Indian man, still with an accent from Mumbai reached out a hand and it turned into a brief hug.

'It's tough John. We're here for you.'

'Thanks. It means a lot.'

He and Tent were soon sitting in the warm sunshine on a bench on the lawn by the harbour. 'Let me have it.' Said John in a parody of how he started a meeting with Clients which Trent found unusual in the circumstances.

'I'd like to talk about the more…substantive matters back in the office.

I thought it would be good to have a coffee in the sunshine but…there are probably only substantive matters to talk about right now unless we wanted to skirt around the edges. Neither of us are like that though are we John?' His tone was apologetic.

'It was…you know…thoughtful to want to do this Trent. Maybe we take these back.'

Once settled in Trent led off. 'I imagine you'll agree things have got to change. You've had a very difficult time and for that reason alone we need to make adjustments, at least in the medium term. And I should mention if you want some help, we can organise that at another practice so you're not speaking with colleagues.'

'I know the way this looks Tent…'

'Let's be clear. This is not the way something looks John. It's the way it is. Whether it's bad luck or technique what does Sunny makes it four?'

'Technique?'

'Can you stand back from this for a minute and see how this effects other people, and yes, the business. Your colleagues who provide other services to these people.

The government agency who contracts with us to supply services for this Program. And yes, a business which people own and put into my hands to run and you're hands to make function.'

'I'm that far off the mark?'

'You want me to lie to you John? Sugar coat things. That's what you want? Let you hide behind the latest suicide because you're vulnerable right now. Even if it's a random pattern it is a pattern and it needs to be taken seriously. Christ, we're talking about people's lives here. I would have thought you'd be the first who would be suggesting you take a break from this side of the business.'

'So I'm going to be working with frog phobia patients now?'

'When did you get so arrogant John. People who have a debilitating fear, if not a terror, of a part of their lives living in their gardens…that's beneath you? You have to have the high risk, vulnerable patients? Well your batting average isn't very good. And I interview a percentage of the patients with a government contract to ensure we're fulfilling our commitments. A lot of the things you talk about are nowhere in the literature. The things you are doing for them or facilitate for them are beyond the scope of our intended relationship and certainly the level of communication they have with you is well beyond the fundamental professional separation which is mandated, and for good reason. It's only in the recent past that I've had sufficient conversations about this with your patients and then I went on leave and when I got back I was very busy so speaking with you about this kept getting pushed back. I very much regret that now.'

'I can lay it out in much more detail, but I'd rather put down a series of brief paragraphs of what needs to change. It would also contain the scope for your reassignment. We'd work together on this, but it would include some of the activities you used to be proactive about such as visits to hospitals, prisons and nursing homes.'

John looked into space. 'You're being very understanding Trent. Sorry I came across the way I did. I don't have an argument with anything you've said and I'm grateful for what you've offered. How long?'

'A month off. Then part time for another month.'

'That's fair. I'll try to get my objectivity back and I'll completely trust your assessment. If you don't think I've achieved that you can extend the part time stipulation. I'll be fine with what you decide in terms of reassignment. I've let my family relationships slip because I was spending too much time on the kind of activities you've described.'

His tone changed because in spite of all he'd said he very much wanted one thing. 'At the risk of flushing my commitment to objectivity down the toilet...' Though this was a thing he was going do even without permission. '...I would really appreciate is if I could go to...identify her remains.'

Trent let out a big sigh. 'You know we don't do that. I met her, interviewed her. Nice kid. She had a great deal of respect for you and was very grateful for all of the things you weren't supposed to be doing for her. And John...I don't want to...diminish the human dimension you showed to her. However as you know when a patient throws themselves off a bridge, we don't usually get involved in that part of it. For good reason.'

'I know we're not supposed to Trent. I...cared about her. I'll be taking time off. The people she's with either won't have their act together to do it or even worse it will be very traumatic for them. One last thing.'

Trent was conflicted. 'Do this last thing. Your appointments have been cleared. Go home and forget everything about psychology for a while.' John got up shook Trent's and went to clean out his office. He left his desk cleared for the temp who would be working there the next day.

He made a call and drove to the police station first as the detective who answered said he'd appreciate it if he could see John before he took him down to the morgue personally.

Soon after John was invited into his office. 'I'm Detective Bruxton.' He reached out his hand and gave John's a firm shake. 'Good to meet you John. It got me curious when I was told where you worked. We have consulting psychologists and an internal guy who's usually off on stress leave. Not that I blame him. I can't get much sense out of that side of the Department lately and I thought you might be interested to look over a case or two. Completely contrary to our many policies and procedures of course.'

'That's what makes it fun.'

'There's some the best analysis I've received lately right there.'

John liked Bruxton right off the bat. Despite the appearances he sometimes contrived, he liked doing his job. Not always the way he was supposed to. He didn't have a partner.

'In days gone by it was simple crimes of passion or about money.' He shook his head. 'Wife banging neighbour. Bang. Drugs didn't equal the weight paid for. Bang. But now we have all of these new age homicides. Young people have been watching TV series or documentaries or streaming commissioned crap that have these improbable serial killer plots. And the killer has some weird motif and terrorises a village or draws in the lead investigator, who has some problems in his past into a strange relationship. Yeah. It gets personal. Often with subtitles.'

'So now we get crimes that are life mimicking art. A TV feedback loop.' They had walked through a locked door. 'Exhibit A. This killer kidnaps some poor homeless guy, I guess they assume no one's going to miss him. Then they cut off the right hand and leave the body someplace easy to find. But the hand goes on a photo journey like a fucking stolen gnome on holiday. And we're supposed to figure out the meaning of it all by where these slowly decomposing hands have their adventures. We have four on tour at the moment. Once the press connects the dots, which I try to not to let them do, I imagine we'll have a 'Handyman Killer' on our...hands.' He laughed at his unintended word choice. 'And this is the other one. I can't come up with a better name yet. This is the Dice Killer.'

'What are they made of?' John recoiled at the cubes with faces ten centimetres along each edge which he could see through a glass freezer door.

'Human skin covering high quality steak. But there's a metal frame of a cube the skin is stitched onto to keep the thing in shape; nice and tight. Then it gets tattooed. Only one face for each cube has dots on it. We have dice number one, two, three and four.' John was going to mention that a single dice is called a 'die' but thought why be pedantic. 'Should be easy to get some leads but the killer has treated the stuff with something so that the DNA is degraded.'

Bruxton looked at John as if he might have a ready answer. 'So what am I looking for here? Pissed off problem gambler. Disaffected croupier. I have no ideas and I wish I didn't need to have any. Why don't these pricks bury them or dissolve them in acid or set their feet in concrete and throw them in the harbour like in the good old days. We solve sixty percent of murder cases. And that's what I hate about these TV inspired murders. If we can't solve a case when some nobody disappears; everybody's okay with that. But when there's a few travelling hands or a freezer full of human dice it's a problem. Dice made of nobodies probably, but it's a thing you have to spend time on.

I wish we were in America and some dickhead in a suit would come marching in with a badge and say something like We're taking over this investigation. This is our turf now. I'd say 'be my guest you wankers'. I'd rather work on a straightforward rape case and put a guy in jail. Or a murder where it's only a matter of figuring out which family member did it.'

John smiled. He didn't think Bruxton was looking for serious professional comment at that time. 'Your weird shit is definitely weirder than mine. As a psychologist I don't know how much I can offer. I'm happy to join the cast of quirky individuals trying to figure things out while the clock is ticking. As it happens, I'm taking leave, and my wife can only stand so much of me. Lately that's measured in the seconds per day.'

'I nearly had a few wives like that. They developed that perspective before we could tie the knot though. I could use some informal, unauthorised, below the radar and insightful ideas that could be arrived at by only one person because of their unique backstory.'

John laughed. 'I'm your man.' His patients liked John so much because he had no pretence and didn't want or expect any from anyone else. 'I'll give theses some thought.

If I think I have something worth talking about, it can be an off the record phone call. Even if it's some noir serial killer name options?'

That caused them to come up with a few names and both laughed and were surprised how many stupid names they could generate off the cuff.

'I'll take you over to where we keep the dead people that haven't been turned into dice.'

John's mood became sombre remembering the purpose of his visit. But as they walked along, he provided a some thoughts on the 'Dice Killer'. 'The dice mean nothing Bruxton. They're used to see if it will bamboozle the people on the side of the law, that also watch TV series and movies and read books on twisted serial killers. They're a red herring. He or she want people to look where there's nothing to find. And so distract them for what the killer is really up to as much as possible. The travelling hand guy, or girl, is playing the classic cat and mouse routine with detectives they also see on TV and in books. Unlike the Dice Killer, they might be leaving hard to find tell-tale clues. It may be that there are fingerprints left from these hands in areas important to the victim or the killer within some radius of the photograph.'

'Interesting perspective about the Dice guy. These Handyman asshole kills random old homeless people so if they're leaving clues it will be to do with the killer.' He shook his head. 'Anyway.' He nodded. 'I think you're right on the Dice Killer. The media will start calling him that once the news gets out and they'll expect us to be doing what you've suggested the killer wants us to do. Looking in the wrong places and wasting time. At a sixty percent solve rate, you can burn only so much time on a case and you have to move on. After that we hand it on to the Cold Case Department full of misfits and older detectives trying to navigate a world that's grown foreign to them. Unfortunately that Department doesn't exist.' Bruxton thought a while and nodded again. John sensed Bruxton may do better than sixty percent because he listened to anyone. That's probably why bodies, or dice, mounding up in his case files were getting to him. 'Fingerprints. I think we could cast a wider net. We've got UV and some of the locations we believe the snapshots were taken might be near handrails or other places a fingerprint might be left. How about I ask the boss if you can be a consulting head reader. I guess you're not allowed to moonlight.'

'I'd be interested. It can be gratis.'

'We have the budget John.' Bruxton said, as he used his magnetic key to get through the last door. 'Our man in the dead person management game is behind in his record keeping so there will be a bit of stainless-steel door bingo if you could turn away John.' John appreciated the courtesy of not having him exposed to seven or eight doors open until he found the right toe-tag. Then he heard him draw the carrier back and leave it out. Bruxton came around and put a light, consoling arm on John's shoulder before he approached the covered remains. 'Your boss called and filled me in John.' At times like this, for all his bluster, Bruxton put being a human in front on being a Detective. 'She...there's no other way to say this John...she went face first. Which is unusual. My recommendation is I leave that part of the young lady's body covered and see if you can identify her somehow else.'

'Sure. And thanks.' They walked over. 'I would never believe this girl was going end up here from what I saw yesterday. She was getting the best of her demons, slowly. Getting a new job. Lived in a managed house that was functional.' When John realised Bruxton was going to move the sheet away from some of Sunny's naked body he put his hand out. 'She loved rings and had a tattoos on her forearm. If that's good enough. He drew her right hand from under the sheets. Each finger had one or two gold plated or silver rings. Some wide, with edging and patterns, some narrow. None of them were especially valuable but she had an eye for good quality, cheap jewellery. So much so that she'd been mugged a few times for it. John pulled her hand into his and squeezed it. He could not bring himself to believe she would do this. Not now. He looked up to see Broxton's eyes on their clasped hand. 'I'm sorry. Probably not supposed to do that. Never once held her hand when she was alive. Wasn't allowed to then either.'

'Don't worry. What I see family going through John…it's heartbreaking.' He swallowed and his eyes even started to water. 'They want to climb right in there with them. Hold them in their arms. They don't want to let them go. I tell them I wish this didn't need to be a memory.' He sighed. 'I only meet them when they're dead.' He shook his head. 'Other times case workers, Parole Officers, Prison Guards and people like yourself John. They're the only ones who come. No family. No friends that are going to come near a policeman. You people work with them. Help them. Care about them. So I know this is important. And tough. When it's a murder. And you hear what the person was like from the family. When they were still walking around. A good person. It can be quite a motivator.'

John knew Bruxton would be as motivated on those cases he dismissed as 'people nobody cared about' as anyone else.

Bruxton breathed out heavily. 'You know John, now that I've seen her, and heard what you said, it doesn't sit right with me. Who goes in headfirst. And, not into the water. She was above a pylon.'

'Yeah.' John had not thought about it. 'Not the pose you're likely to adopt jumping off a bridge. I don't think people think much about the landing until they jump or let go. And that's about the time I'd say regret kicks in.'

'People might still have their feet down or fall sideways, forwards, backwards it doesn't matter their head usually cracks. Or it's a disorganised mess. Most people don't jump from that bridge because it's not high enough to give them the 'concrete' effect when they hit the water. So your girl's all juiced up on booze and pills and jumps off the lower end of the bridge and aims for a concrete platform surrounding a pillar. That's what the report said. I'd have to go and refresh my memory, but those pillars don't extent far past the railing of the bridge.'

'Sunny never drank, took pills, not even weed. She was a heroin girl. Meth for a while. When she was clean, she was completely clean. Clean when she left my office. Maybe she got back on it last night, but I'll bet my car the autopsy will say she was clean.'

They started back for Bruxton's office. 'I'm not going win the much coveted 'Detective of the Week' award by converting a suicide to a murder but next week…I'll put a couple of hours aside to go through the file. In the meantime I'll look at the bloodwork for the girl…Sunny. See what she was on. If anything.'

'Yeah. Thanks for your help Bruxton.'

'Thanks for your ideas on the TV Crime Froot Loops. Happy to hear more.'

John parked at the small garden area with a playground connecting to another park via footpath under the bridge. It didn't take too long to find the place Bruxton had told him the body was found. He looked down and he could see an oval bloodstain on the edge of a concrete pylon footing. He believed he could land on it. But he would need to climb over the rails and position himself right over the narrow place where the pylon footing extended past the rail. He'd need to drop straight off and turn in the air to face down. At nighttime she couldn't see the water let alone the footing of a pylon. He knew her mind. And it simply didn't work that way. Certainly not if she was wasted.

His boss's words came to mind. 'throw themselves off a bridge.' But people can't throw themselves. They can either jump or fall. They need to be thrown. He looked around the area of the rails and after a few minutes of careful scrutiny of the pavement and all of the railings, he saw a hair in a crack where the main structure connected to the handrail. And another one caught between joins in the main frame nearby. John could imagine someone lifting Sunny up over the handrail and dropping her over. Bumping her head on the support next to the rail. Probably not even intending to let her hit the pylon footing, rather deliver another overdosed drowned junkie to an overworked police department. Now he knew they would find heroin in Sunny's body. And it was a jolt to John to suddenly realise who put it there.

His phone rang. 'Where the fuck are you John? We're leaving for the school in fifteen minutes. You were going to be home to drive us over there.' He knew Patrice had been on a slow burn to an explosion for a long time. This was probably going to be it. She had been looking forward to the play and, by agreement, having a few drinks at intermission.

'Something…really bad happened and I had some things I needed to do. I'm on my way now.'

'John these days something bad is always happening. Well guess what. Missing your daughter's production is something really bad. But it's not important to you, compared to almost everything else'

'Okay. Yes. I'm on my way.'

'You're still in the city?'

'I'll be there when it starts.' He was running.

'Sure you will.' Patrice had taken her unhappiness with her husband up a notch. And there weren't any notches left.

'Hi dad.' He heard in the background before the line went dead. As he had done so many times, he thanked the Lord their last child was who she was.

He ran towards the carpark but looked behind himself frequently for an empty cab. That would give him an alibi. One came along after a few minutes and though the cabbie didn't want to stop on the bridge he put on his hazard light and motioned John to run, which he did. He took off quickly amid air full of honking.

'Thanks mate.' John gave him the address.

'Glad I pulled over. That's a nice fare.'

'How much extra to get there as fast as you can without breaking any laws.'

'Twenty more should do it.'

'Here's fifty. I'm probably going to be late for my daughter's big night and my wife's going to skin me alive.' The cab's speed was building. How he didn't get pulled over John wasn't sure. The lights were only going down when he arrived. John was going to take note of some memorable moments at the start of the play the discuss them on the way home to provide evidence to his daughter he was there from the beginning.

However, having crossed a threshold, there would be not mollifying Patrice. 'Nice you could make it.'

'Sorry.'

That was the limit of the exchange. John was going to make himself as small a target as possible. At intermission, there was some comment as to why he hadn't driven home. He said he needed a taxi because there had been some issues, unspecified, with his car which was why he was late.

He told the circle listening how much he'd paid the taxi driver to do anything he could to get him there. 'Just in time.'

On the way home, in order to build up his credentials as an involved parent, he talked a lot about the strengths of the production and the people who made it happen. Skilful as he thought he was, it didn't occur to him that he dominated the interaction with their daughter. He and Hazel were soon laughing. Sometimes about things that her mother believed they 'shouldn't be laughing about'. Leaving Patrice unable to break in on some topics. But the day was catching up with John.

The weight of the other suicides had been building. Sunny had been special, and she'd shown every sign that she could climb out of the pit she'd been thrown into. And broken down into the simplest human emotion, he'd liked her. He tried to hold all of this back as he gave his daughter a congratulatory hug. But it started to come out and she let him know it was okay to literally cry on her shoulder. Soon he was crying and sobbing, like he hadn't done in years. Whether he was allowed to feel it or not, Sunny had been special to him. What she'd come through was unimaginable, yet she had a big generous heart and was willing to look inside herself in order to get better.

He went to get a beer and saw Patrice was pouring a glass of wine. He was immediately caught in a no-win situation. If he nodded pleasantly and took it somewhere, anywhere, to actually enjoy it, this would be unforgivable. If he drew up a chair, there was a tirade on its way and it wasn't really going to be modified by heartfelt apologies nor, on this occasion, some justifiable excuses. The impact of his excuses had been exhausted.

'It's all about you John. Big night for our daughter and you're dumping some shit on her she's too young to deal with. She'll pretend she is; but she's just a kid. Or it would be nice if she could be.'

'I apologise. It was a…tough day.'

'Yes John. I can never compete with your tough days. I can bring home a story about some kid who had nits. Or one of the hair dryers fucked up. But you've got the kid who watched his parents barbequed in their house, or your patient gets high and he's holding a knife at police. They get it off him and shoot him anyway. And you keep rolling it out there onto the dinner table. Good therapy.'

'Sure. Message received. Keep work at work.'

'You think I believe that shit John. Tell me. Did you lose your phone yesterday.' He pulled his phone out of his pocket as evidence he had it but he knew he was in trouble. Big trouble. 'Not that phone John. The 'secret' phone. Oh. Look. It somehow got into my bag.'

Her voice grew icy. 'I used to think it was so sweet that every single device you have had our wedding anniversary as the code. But as time went by, and you forget our anniversary, for two years straight now because I haven't reminded you, I realise it's just a number which unlocks what you really want. Your little circle of devotees to which you are the psychologist guru come to save them.'

John knew he wasn't going to like what was about to happen. It was only a matter of degree. 'And look at this. Six people. Patients. The only contacts. Let's open up the text messages from one at random. A text a day, may be two. Confirming an off the books appointment. Phone calls. Twenty minutes on a Thursday evening when you could have been at home. Oh, and shortly after that a phone call from another patient. Half an hour.'

'Do you know how I know what's going on in detail. It's not because I picked up your phone today. It's because our phone accounts are held by my business. Contract hairdresser for hire. Not exciting. Or is it?

I have our phones and all the kids phones in a tax deductable little bundle. I've never seen you use your personal phone in years because the work phone is all you use. Then I looked at those bills they email. Yeah. The itemised bills. So I went to our telco and waited around. They said a teenager could help me, but I said I wanted to wait for the older woman serving someone. I told her what I wanted. She could guess why, and she told me as the account holder I could have whatever I damn well pleased. So I got this.' She held up a late model smartphone. 'There wasn't a name for it so we called it a mirror phone. It dumps everything from your account, via the cloud into this. We set it up so that there is no way I could bump it and make a call or open an app. I can only look at call records and texts. Maybe I could have set it up to listen to the calls, but I didn't. Privacy's a big deal for me.'

'Look at this patient, so many characters used on one occasion you had to break up the texts. And John, let's scroll back a bit in that thread of 'out of hours' psychological care. This is my beautiful daughter Hazel. You sent a photograph and the name of our daughter to someone who was living on the streets last year. A fucking heroin addict. Who knows where that information will end up John. Based on all of this back and forward these people could know where we live.

They could be finding out all sorts of information with some innocent questions you'd be too fucking dumb to pick up on. This isn't appropriate John but it's also not Psychology. It's a fucking mix of new age crap, old time philosophy and words used in psychology. I'm not naïve about this stuff. You'll recall where we met. I decided I didn't want to bring home a pile of shit every day. The texts to this girl go on and on. The goddam phone had to buffer to get this far back. How have you been today – Have you tried this – Remember to do this – Give me a call if you need to and on and fucking on.'

'Now John. Let's read a string of recent texts between you and I. She opened her phone. 'Do we need anything from the store.' The next night. 'I'll be home late. Sorry I thought the rehearsal was tomorrow. Can you take her, or maybe a cab. I will pick her up.' And look. 'Fish sounds great. I'm running late so start without me.' Here's a tender moment. 'I can't find my iPad. Have you seen it at home?' That's us John. Pretty boring compared to your alter ego.'

He nodded. 'You've got great timing Patrice. I was brought to the realisation today I've gone way overboard as a clinician. For what I thought were the right reasons.'

'But based on what happened today…I've realised; I've had it demonstrated to me, that I've only managed to fuck everything up. Everything.' He had fucked things up for Sunny and the others in a totally different way from the way Patrice and his boss thought. He wasn't going to sit there at take this deluge of shit though. Like it was worth nothing that he'd cared about some people. And the ones many people called losers. 'Your response to your 'concerns' about me was to hack into my private life, which married people are still supposed to be allowed to have, or so I thought. Instead of showing me what you thought was wrong, you voyeuristically look at this stuff for what; weeks, months. Nice one Patrice I wasn't fucking any of these people. I liked them. I liked all of them and I let my empathy or whatever name you'd rather call it; a self-absorbed idiocy maybe, get way out of hand. Yeah. Was I drifting towards being some kind of fucking guru. Maybe. Read them again and tell me that's what was really happening. But do you know what Patrice. I'd choose my misdemeanours any day over yours. You could have confronted me with this on day one but you didn't.'

'Guilty as charged John. As usual. You're always the nice guy living with the hard to deal with bitch. Sorry…I wanted to spend some time to understand how far back behind number fucking six I really am. I figured it out John. I don't even rate to be on your fucking list. I haven't had this for even two weeks.' She was shaking. It wasn't rage. It was pure pent up emotion of all kinds. 'To see six people in front of me that you share more intimate parts of your life than you've even tried to with me for years. Sure John. It's all my fault because somehow, I'm the one who tried less. And it's hard not to notice that Number One is good looking. A little rough around the edges because of the terrible time she's had. A blonde twenty-two-year-old. I totally accept it's plutonic. But over and over again in the course of months she gets more attention than I ever did any time after that brief honeymoon glow. I know everybody has to say goodbye to that sooner or later. But you've been communicating with her sometimes three times a day.' They both knew much of that were the texts and photos sent out from Sunny to her contact list.

He knew he shouldn't have said the next thing using it to return fire. But he did. 'She's no longer something you need to be concerned with Patrice. She committed suicide last night and that's why I was late. The one and only time I think I had a pretty good excuse. I went to identify her remains.'

Patrice's reaction was not what he'd expected. 'Sunny committed suicide.' There was a very long pause which John knew not to intrude on. 'Irrespective of what you did or how you got there I could see something in that girl as much as you could. We both could see that unless she got into an environment away from the shit part of the city she lived in and stopped mixing with the fucking leaches, it was just going to be a cycle for her eventually.' John was surprised to hear this as a reaction. Patrice had become fascinated by the girl and started to ignore what her husband wrote. She read Sunny's texts and looked at the photos she liked to share. Patrice's comments about her age and looks were convenient jabs at a man who seemed to think his apologies meant something anymore. There were not very many pictures of Sunny herself but a lot of the places she went to and the friends she had. Tears started to trickle down Patrice's face. 'Believe it or not I was going to ask if that girl could come live with us for a while. Yeah. Once I got through dealing out what I thought would be some cathartic punishment to someone I have become convinced does not give a shit about me anymore. She could have broken free, I know it. I could have easily given her a training job. I know Hazel would've liked her.'

He shrugged. 'It's not really allowed…with a patient.'

When Patrice threw the phone at him, it wasn't an irritable toss. It was a draw your arm back to near the full extent and lash it forward. During this process she was shouting 'And this fucking is?' The phone connected with his forehead. The corner hitting just above his right eye. Patrice didn't show the slightest bit of concern. 'I'd been waiting. Waiting for the last few weeks. Maybe you'd do the right thing. Maybe you would tell me the truth. Or god forbid you would tell…' Patrice was angry, but also crying. '…tell just one of these people that you were so close to, that you had a wife, a partner in your life. And that she had even one redeeming quality. That I might get the tiniest mention as a bit player in your life. But I'm nothing John. Nobody. But for a while we had something, someone we cared about on that phone in common. And all you can throw at me is a piece of procedural shit you've flouted every day for years.'

He was totally spent, and now he knew he had brought a terrible risk way beyond anything Patrice could conceive within their orbit. His phone was on the floor below the kitchen bench. He nodded towards it. 'Keep it. They're nearly all gone.'

'Gone?' Patrice was suspicious. 'To another program.' Patrice hoped that was the answer.

'Matty's going to be reassigned to another psych in our office. The others…'

'John… please don't tell me five of the contacts in that phone…'

'Four. Toby dropped out eight months ago.' John had decided Toby wasn't deserving of his various extracurricular activities. It had saved his life. 'But yeah. It looks that way.'

'It looks that way? What the fuck kind of answer is that. How could the practice be…allowing this?'

John wished he had not been so foolish as to provide that detail. 'They've responded to it. I'm having some time off then part time. I'm going to be reassigned.'

'I need some time to process this John.'

'Patrice, right now, I'm not too interested in whether you process this or not. What I'm going to do, is to prepare a big list of the things I've got wrong, and it won't be short, and you can correct it, add to it, whatever you want. I'll work through it.' He got up to leave. 'But can you please stop shouting at me and throwing things. Maybe that's why I'm not as affectionate as you'd like me to be.'

He went and sat out on the veranda in the dark with another beer. 'Hey.'

He was so on edge he jumped at the sound of his almost seventeen-year-old daughter Hazel, still in her medieval maiden's costume because she didn't want to take it off. 'There's children in the house you know.' She smiled. She loved her dad though he barely did anything to deserve it. She was at odds with her mother who did everything wrong trying to hold onto it. She had a wicked laugh. 'Don't worry, I don't know what you were talking about; or yelling about. But I did pick up on the general...now what's the right word...' She did this a lot. '...tenor would it be.'

'Well I'm glad it was only a tenor trauma event.'

'Another night with Mum beating up my dad.' She said that ironically and laughed. Then looked across at him, and there was enough light to see a large oval swelling coming up prominently above his eye. 'Holy Shit. She really is beating up on you.' Hazel was concerned now.

'Your mother put her phone down a little...more firmly than she intended, and it bounced off the table.'

'I believe that.'

'Hazel there's something very important I want to tell you about your mother.' Hazel wondered if her father was at long last going to say something bad about Patrice. Which he'd never once done.

'She's never wrong.' There had been frequent tensions between Hazel and her mother. Occasionally developing into arguments between two powerful wills. And the frequency was increasing. 'Yes.' He continued. 'There are some messaging issues.' They both laughed. 'But she's nearly always right in her assessments and those assessments are always made from a perspective as to what's best for you. You're old enough to decide yourself what's best for you but try to appreciate what she's doing is based on generally good judgement and your best interests. The challenge for her is she has to let go of that and give way to your lousy judgements because it's your right to make them. It's going to get much worse now that you're a renowned actress. You're going to become an insufferable prima donna.'

Hazel didn't want a 'your mother's infallible' talk at that time. 'Do you think what I was doing was actressing?' She wanted some honest feedback, but it needed to be couched in a light-hearted cocoon.

'You watch any entertainment involving actors and some will be just acting, it's unconvincing. Others will have disappeared and become the character, and sometimes with a movie you'll have to wait for the credits to realise who it was. And it's only because I'm your father I'll tell you're in the first category. No one else will probably ever say that.'

'You asshole.' Hazel said. Then in an affected thespian voice she followed on with. 'So you don't think I belong in the theeataaa.'

'I think if you go into that vocation there's an exceedingly good chance you'll be very poor. But you should follow you heart.'

She looked him with retaliation on her mind. 'Okay then. Getting back to the difficulties you have playing your part; in your role I mean.' She was pleased to be turning the tables in what she though such an elegant riposte. 'Mum's always right. And she's unhappy with you because…'

'Quite a few things. And her messaging approach was appropriate on this occasion.'

'Well. That being said. Do you need someone to talk this through with. Can't talk to mum as she's one of the combatants. So I think a heart to heart is in order. Take the burden away. Drain the tension. Get it all off your chest.

Soften the sharp edges of the picture and whatever other stuff you charge people fuckloads so they have the privilege of listening to you.'

'That's not going to happen.'

'So all that advice for years from you about talking things through doesn't apply to you.'

'Parenting if nine tenths hypocrisy. Surely you've figured that one out by now.'

'So the takeaway for me from all this is my father is a hypocrite and confirms he has been an unavailable parent intentionally, I can't act for shit, my mother is worth listening to because my judgement is woeful and I should be old enough to look past her latent hostility and it would now appear; violent tendencies.'

'I'd do some minor edits at the end but…the acting thing is not true. You're exactly what I described in the second characterisation. You can disappear and become the character. However. I said what I did initially because if you can't accept criticism and believe in yourself, you're going to crash and burn whether you're any good or not.'

'Wow. I have no idea what to believe now. Given that little pearl of wisdom was after the nine tenths hypocrisy thing; I'm exhausted. Parental shouting, domestic violence and hypocrisy has wilted this tender flower. I suppose you'll be continuing to flitter in and out of our lives, the main cause of mum's hostility which I bear the brunt of by the way because I'm the only target here most of the time.'

'How did that obnoxious fifteen-year-old become a thespian and faux insightful nearly seventeen-year-old. I'll be home for a month because of…work issue…and I'm planning to be here every day when you get home from school. And hence I think things will turn to shit for you and I because the ships in the night thing has worked so well for us for years. My focus is going to be on your mother, whom I have been a complete asshole to for those very same years. And you, young lady, will start to be the focus of an implacable and united parental will. Ruthless discipline will be the new management strategy for our wilful and wayward daughter.'

'Oh Paleeese. We shall see what we shall see. And I don't 'get home from school' much these days dad. That's a child thing. And oh yeah. I carry around condoms in my schoolbag. Get over it. Ha. I would love to come up against any paltry ruthless discipline you two come up with.

It would hone my skills as a comic actor.' She kissed him goodnight as she was saying this. She walked towards her room but then turned and went into the lounge. She leaned into the figure standing next to the curtain by the open window to the veranda. In a very quiet whisper her father couldn't hear she said. 'Night mum.'

John was at the breakfast table early having set out a nice spread, but not overdoing it. Hazel's lunch was packed. In a box no one could see though. Both Hazel and Patrice knew it would have foods Hazel was not usually allowed to take for lunch. They sat together after a 'coffee time' order was filled for his daughter.

'Soooo. I'm on stress leave. Or more like please keep away from the office for a month leave, and then I'm part time for a while. My plan is to do my share, for once, and be here to help with breakfast and be home by the time someone very special gets home. That being my loving partner. Maybe have canapes ready or at least have dinner started. In between those times, I may tidy up the farm. I'm ready to move on and sell it if only said partner would let me.'

'Dad. Can you not see the phone near mum's hand.' There was a slightly frosty silence. Hazel looked from one to the other. 'What. Too soon?'

John's pronouncements had solicited eye rolling from Patrice at the farm reference. She had never wanted 'the farm' comprised of an old shed and a few paddocks surrounded by dairy farms.

Hazel arose theatrically and smiled. 'I'll have to bid you both a fond farewell unfortunately. I'll take my leave while you two continue to indulge yourselves in such lighthearted banter.' She swept from the room.

As she departed John said. 'Our first breakfast together and it's going well.' He looked at Patrice 'That daughter of ours eh? Where did we go wrong with number three?'

Patrice dragged out the best smile she could manage at what was a painful and confusing juncture in her life and said. 'It's more a case of how we managed to get it so right.' John thought it a shame their daughter had left the room.

John was also caught off guard. He wasn't used to sincerity, by anyone at the kitchen table.

'Yes… Anyhow, if not at the farm, or here doing some cleaning for once, I'll be in the city, very occasionally, doing some things in case anyone wants anything or needs a lift. I am considering leaving my job in town and getting something in a small clinic out here, or maybe working from home. Decisions which would be taken via a process we went through as a family to ascertain what's best for all.' But then he added quickly. 'But mainly with my partner. In all things'

All the time he'd been saying this she found it hard to take her eyes off the prominent egg sized lump caused by her phone assault the evening before.

'I'm off to the city. Recover the car. Leave the dishes. I'll address that issue when I return.' There was a swift unexpected peck on his wife's cheek.

As he reached the door he heard. 'What happened to us John.'

It broke through into his mind. He remembered her. Why he dated her, fell in love with her, married her. And then he'd gradually taken her for granted until that girl, who did have a sense of humour, who was tender, and loving had become something she never wanted to be. He walked back to her and dragged out the most sincere smile he'd shared with her in years. He held out his hand and she took it and he drew her up. 'I did Patrice. I happened to us.' He looked into her eyes which rarely occurred now. 'Give me a chance.'

John had reached the car after again visiting the place on the bridge he had been the afternoon of the day before. There was a hefty fine for parking overnight. The phone rang. 'John. Bruxton. I'm going on a visit for an investigation. Another dead hand of fate has come to rest on my shoulder. and I'm passing where the unfortunate young lady was found. Thought we could look it over from the railings. If you want to keep going for a crime scene visit in the wilderness you would get a stripe on the junior detective badge.'

'Sounds great. If you like I can meet you at the carpark at the base on the city side.'

'Twenty.' Bruxton liked brevity.

John had thought Bruxton would walk with him to the pylon, but he picked him up and drove up next to the place and put a blue flashing light on top of the car. 'Blue light. People slow down. Maybe wave anxiously. Everyone is wondering how much I know as they pass by. If they look really guilty, I pull them over. They take me to the body.

I rough them up a little and knock off early because of job well done. All because they looked guilty.'

'It's similar in my job. Someone comes in. I say they have no problems compared to my problems and they pay exorbitant fees to listen to how I've managed to completely screw my life up and they piss off. We both feel better because they made me feel better and so they figure things can't be as bad as they thought. It wears off after a few hours, but they, or the government, and hence you as a taxpayer have already paid. I don't give a shit. I knock off early. In my case I play FreeCell in the office till late, so I have to spend less time with a wife who hates me.'

'A time-honoured strategy. I almost needed to employ it twice.'

John was caught short. He'd been making jokes without being sensitive to his apparent statistics. One of which they were now looking down at as a brown stain. Bruxton was genuine but it was too hard to live that way all day in his job. They both changed the mood to something they knew Sunny deserved. Bruxton was methodically studying all along the railings, on the footpath but came up with nothing.

John hadn't expected they'd visit and hoped the detective didn't pick up on the mild scent of dilute antiseptic he'd used at specific locations on the railings. He'd collected Sunny's hair and put in in a little zip lock bag.'

They were on the road again. 'Crime scene time.'

Bruxton didn't have much to say unless it was necessary information or being cynical and sarcastic, so they drove in silence. As they approached a parking area leading to some tracks in a National Park Bruxton said. 'This is the first jaunt for the hand of the fifth victim of Handyman Killer. I can't come up with a better name and it's grown on me. Some good work from the GIS and drone guys got us to where the hand had its first holiday snap taken. We found some DNA where the hand had been and it matched the one in the photo of one the unwilling amputee resting in in peace behind one of those silver doors. No one has claimed any of these guys. No one really knows them, even when you talk to as many homeless people you can find. It's sad.'

'Little hint. The law and homeless people. Oil and water. They don't mix. They don't know anything about anything because they want you to go away. They have a dozen or more reasons you could throw them in a cell. For most of them nothing good ever came into their lives via a copper.'

'Ouch. Maybe I should start up one of those reality TV shows like where rich assholes are sent out to be homeless for a week. This would be senior sergeants and detectives. We'd all be crying for our mother on the first night. Or I could send you out to talk to them because you can't arrest them.'

'Yes. But I do seem to have somewhat of a knack of causing people having a hard time in life to commit suicide' John questioned himself. How heartless had he become.

'Hey John. They're homeless. Who gives a shit. On a slow day I go brutalise them and arrest them to keep my mind busy.' Bruxton was on solid ground. With someone who understood him. That was a short list. His mind confronted that fact. Then turned to other things. 'Back to the matter at hand. The little splash of DNA would be all we had to go on, again, except for your idea about fingerprints. It's nearly a kilometer back down the track to a suspension bridge. The guy with the UV kit was only calibrating it in with his own prints and running along the rail to see what the typical smudging of lots of users leave. He wanted to see what a neat set of prints looked like with his toy so he went to a metal tube that's slid over the braided wire anchored to the ground to hold up the bridge support. He came across this.'

Braxton pulled a photocopy out of his coat pocket. There were five fingerprints. When John looked closely, he could see they were five thumb prints. From his low base of knowledge it looked like they were from five different people. After a ten minute walk up the trail they approached the piece of painted metal tubing of the suspension bridge support which was off the track. Police were searching the area. 'I'll show you the gadget. Technology is pretty advanced these days.'

'Should he be here?' Came a voice off to the left.

Bruxton turned and said mildly. 'We're here because of him. Anyway, I'm going to take him to the next here, so he won't be here. He'll be there.'

John was concerned Bruxton was getting himself into trouble. 'Who was that?'

'Him? He's my boss. We have this fun play fighting thing going on. You know; we have the old 'pretend to disrespect each other' back and forward. At least I hope that's how he sees it. Haven't had a pay rise in years now that I think about it.'

Bruxton asked the man with the machine to put it over the area and the prints came up clearly. They had been very carefully pressed onto the metal. John studied the prints. He said. 'Officer, amazing job finding this crucial evidence. Would it be okay to turn the light on and off or move it to the side a few times.'

'No worries.' Came the reply from someone who didn't get praise or called Officer often and appreciated it when it happened.

'There's a tiny chance you don't need the hands because I think they've put these prints here like a treasure hunt.' John gave Bruxton a subtle look that it would be good they could talk alone. Which Bruxton conveyed to the officer, apparently believing that being unnecessarily blunt to your colleagues kept policing interesting.

John picked up a twig and keeping it well away from the railing pointed it to a location on the metal above and below the prints at the far end and said. 'You see those tiny little clean areas on the tubing above and below the two outside prints. It looks they made marks there, probably with a soft pencil and then carefully cleaned them away. The outside prints are slightly angled. I think if you put a protractor with the base at the lower dot it would give you and angle to the upper dot.

You would have two lines that intersect somewhere in that direction. Maybe there would be another clue like this near where another hand had a holiday snap was taken. Four prints maybe. That's my guess. Maybe the number of prints continues falling closer to home. I don't think they expect you to find this. It's serial killer aficionado stuff. They probably boast about it to their serial killer friends. Like that Dice guy. They have drinks on Wednesdays. Talk about how dumb the cops are. Brainstorm their next pathetic motif.'

'Your theory about this clue seems pretty straightforward. However…I do have a question of a technical nature. What's a protractor?' In this case Bruxton actually didn't know, or more accurately had forgotten what a protractor was.

'Bruxton, interacting with your colleagues about this would bring out a crippling social anxiety in me. That's why I became a psychologist. You know. Physician heal thyself. It didn't work. But I make a lot of money being bad at it so who cares? What I'm meaning here is don't mention my name in terms of this crazy theory. I don't want to be seen as foolish when the whole protractor thing turns out to be ridiculous. Once that occurs, looking foolish would be your role.'

'Remind me what a protractor is so I get it right and I'll take the risk. I'll call it in on the way back and get one of the boffins to look at it. The trouble's going to be the scale. Do the lines cross in a hundred meters or ten kilometres?'

John really started to think he'd missed his calling. 'By the look of the dots, they will cross not very far from the metal tubing. You know this freak might be into bush walking based on what the bodiless hands get up to. If you got a bunch of topographic maps of different scales and put the protractor lines on each it would give you three or four possible distances. It will show you a relationship to where the other hands were photographed or if locations were never identified; what surfaces are within fifty meters to a kilometer of where the lines cross that would make fingerprints. Someone into orienteering would love this, when they're not watching streaming formula crime shows. I think they're doing it on your patch because you know you fit the mould pretty well as the curmudgeonly detective.'

'I think that's a compliment right. I don't want to say that word because I might pronounce it wrong and look stupid. It doesn't mean that I'm stupid does it?'

'I'm pretty sure it means relentless, clever and maybe uncompromising. Even if it means you have to cut across the grain.'

'I have a dictionary you know John.'

'Really?'

'Christ you know me so well. This is getting spooky. I can go and buy one you know.'

'But you'll soon rationalise that you don't really care that much and it's not going to change you so why waste the money.'

'Yep.'

'Now you know what curmudgeonly means.'

'Yeah. Actually I've decided that's not even a real word. It's Head Doctor mind games. Which was fun while it lasted. Anyhow let's get away from all the police around here. They make me feel guilty even though I haven't done anything wrong.'

Later a protractor was acquired and he asked the boffins to go to a mapping store to get each different scale of map for the area. Especially what orienteering types might use. He said he'd be calling his Trainee Detective when he needed him.

John had a lot to do. The four suicides had a significant intersection in John's life beyond being his patients. Finding the evidence Sunny had been murderer was initially a relief that he hadn't caused his patients to kill themselves. However it was short line of reasoning to realise he had in fact killed them. By association.

However he was primarily going to become a model father and husband but somehow achieve this without antagonising Patrice by being better at…anything…than she was. For two weeks he spent time each day gathering evidence about the improbable number of suicides during his watch. He spent two days at the farm, getting it ready for sale, and one day cleaning the house within an inch of its life. On the Friday of the second week he came home to very thick air. Patrice had tried to venture into an area she thought motherly advice was entirely appropriate. She had miscalculated the acceptability of the topic from Hazel's perspective. From there Patrice had eventually and unwisely migrated to what was really preoccupying her. That Hazel loved her father more than her.

Hazel had a bit of wisdom to offer on the topic. 'Let's share a perspective on this mum. Things would be fine if you didn't deny your pathetic insecurities by pretending to be secure and confident around someone you think is dumb enough to believe it. The next step might be for you to cheer the fuck up. If you think you're going to get me to carry your shit bag around guess what; I've decided that I'm going to be nobody's shit wagon because if I do that once, there's plenty of people around wanting to load me up. If you don't want me here, I know of a dive with a crack whore position or positions; available.'

John couldn't relay much of what he was up to, so the meal was being consumed in awkward silence. Bruxton called. While it was ringing he said. 'Call from a Detective about a serial killer, anyone want to take it.'

'Sure.' Said Patrice. She took the phone and answered 'This is Patrice. I'm John's wife. He asked if someone with some intelligence should take the call.'

'Intelligence. How about we add stunning beauty, big heartiness and saintly patience to that. Along measured and strategic violence when and where appropriate. I've seen the evidence as to how you keep John in line when he needs it. But I've also heard all about your model looks sitting side by side with an almost otherworldly sincerity.' This was all too much for Patrice after the afternoon she'd had. Hazel swiped the phone from his mother's hand.

'I'm here also Detective. I'm smarter then both of my parents combined by a factor of three so I may be able to help. I'll encourage them to be quiet while we sort this one out. But I'll put them on speaker so they can pretend to be 'involved parents' while I do something I love but they'll never understand.'

'I can see my force of assistant detectives expanding by the minute. Your father had an idea, shortly before I would have had it, and way slower than you would have figured it out. We got a second location on some serial killers treasure hunt an hour ago. Once we used the right map. Why don't I bring the ladies up to speed John? As long as there's a clear understanding this conversation never happened.'

Patrice and Hazel listened with interest and were surprised what John had been up to and the degree to which he'd been instrumental in helping with the case. There was some back and forward but not much was contributed until Hazel said. 'You might not want to be doing this stuff in daylight or you'll spook them. In daylight you should be heading off in the wrong direction like bumbling idiots. The real path should be followed at night, with people wearing black clothes and their faces painted black.'

'We're not allowed to do that face paint anymore. Balaclava's don't have the face washing problem either. And we also have an effective diversity policy. But I think the rest of your idea is good.'

'Of course I could profile the killers very quickly if you give me all the files.' She said blithely.

'Based on the genes you have I would like to do that. But it's impossible procedurally. However, because of the two, no…it's three breakthrough ideas your family have caused me to have, I can give them to John. But he would be expected to keep them completely secure at all times.'

'I can work with that.' Said Hazel.

'Keep those ideas rolling in people.' Being Bruxton he simply hung up.

'I want those files on my desk by Monday John.' Said Hazel. 'And that's Monday morning. I can see I'm going to have some time off school in service of the greater good here.'

John needed to step up and be the one to take some flack. 'You'll do whatever we tell you to do…young lady.' He looked at Patrice with the I'm sorry I only ever seem to make things worse all the time look.

Patrice looked at both of them. And swallowed. It wasn't easy but she said. 'Family. The Ice Lady is starting thaw. Give me time.' She was trying not to let her damn eyes fill to the brim. 'Give me time.'

'That would be Ice Maiden.' Said John.

John was trying to manage his primary preoccupation. From what he was learning about the apparent suicides of his patients he knew he was running out of time for number five. The deaths had happening to a schedule and always occurred around the same time in the evening. As the time approached John simply said he had to go out for two hours each evening, for an even more confidential law enforcement project. But he would explain everything soon.

He started his vigil just in time. It was the third night. There was only one contact on his 'other' phone left. He hadn't taken that phone back as a demonstration to Patrice things had changed. He kept in touch with the patient, Matty Warren, on his work phone now. Matty had been a patient whose appointments in the Program had run their course four months before. John's communication had wound down to the point he was there if Matty needed him which happened occasionally. A specific person from Matty's past had been the victim of a shark attack and that had improved his state of mind considerably.

A Holden V8 Commodore which had seen better days was parked down the street which suggested to John he may have arrived too late. He parked further away in the other direction so he could still see the front of the house but especially the car. He had the rego and some photographs but would like to confirm who was driving it and follow him home rather than need to track the registration down.

He wasn't going to try to save Matty, which he felt a twinge of guilt about. After an hour he was surprised there had been no movement, so he got out and was going to start to look around. Then he heard a voice behind him. 'Good to see you after so long Johnny Boy. You know who's next after number five.' The words were slightly slurred. John saw the bat coming down. He wasn't able to avoid it entirely but moved aside enough so that it wasn't a crushing blow. The man could have followed through and finished him off. However he didn't want to leave evidence at this location and he wanted John to experience what was going to happen to his family.

As John regained consciousness he fought hard to recover quickly. The Commodore was gone. He got on the phone to his daughter while he started driving and felt a wave of relief when heard her voice. He cut off her greeting. 'Hazel shut up and listen.

I need you to run to the car now and drive. Are you running. Don't ask any questions are you running.'

'Yes. What about mum.'

'She'll fuck you around Hazel. Are you in the car? Drive I'll call mum next. Go into the city and meet some friends. I'll call soon.'

Hazel, on her L plates, passed an old car coming down the quiet street at the base of the Blue mountains where they lived. She was tempted to go back to see where it went however her father had been far too compelling for that.

He called Patrice who was slow to pick up. 'Hazel just left in the car.' She said.

'Shut up and listen Patrice. I want you to run into the bush now. Run. Don't walk.

'John what's happening. What's this…'

'Will you shut up and do what I'm fucking asking for once.'

'I'm putting my shoes on now.'

'Patrice leave your fucking shoes.'

There was a strange combination of sounds and a pause. 'Hi there Johnny Boy.' There was a dark laugh.

'She wriggles around a lot this this one. I think I cracked a tooth when I shoved the gun down her throat.'

John had been roaring towards home, calling Hazel then Patrice as he was becoming airborne on the short rises. 'We should talk Darren. I've got a few things you want. One in particular will make you very happy. The other one will keep you out of prison. I've been following after you and picking up evidence at the crime scenes. Lots of evidence. I can show it to you. For the grand prize, we'll have to discuss that in person. It's better than you think. Have a beer, don't hurt Patrice Darren, she's as innocent as...' The phone went dead.

John stopped the car a hundred meters from the house and ran into the bush. He called out. 'We're going to have a talk first Darren. Go into the lounge. I don't have a weapon.'

'Talk fast you fucking asshole.'

'Like I said Darren. You will do time. A lot of time time if you hurt Patrice. I've collected evidence at all five 'suicides', including Matty tonight, and as you might know I'm friends with a Senior Detective. Everything lands on his desk tomorrow. Including some video of your car at a crime scene tonight. I've got a proposition that gives you what you want, and you go home with nothing to worry about.'

'Go on.' Darren was suspicious. But also had become anxious to find out John had guessed he was behind all the apparent suicides.

'Darren. What happened to…you brother. The effect it all had on your family. I hurt innocent people because of what I did. And now this. Five people Darren. Dead because of what I did all those years ago. Every one of them right on the cusp of getting a second chance. You shoot my wife. Kill my daughter. The bodies are piling up Darren. Of people who don't deserve to die. You go to jail for something I started twenty-five years ago. Believe it or not I'm sick of all this. My wife and daughter are going to hate me now that they know. The Psychologists Board are on the verge taking my licence to practice away already, and I…I hate myself and…it won't go away.'

'So what's your plan Johnny Boy.'

'Here's a proposition. It's simple enough, but it's going have to happen in stages purely so I know Patrice is safe.'

'What's your fucking plan Jonny Boy. Do you think I believe any of that shit.'

'I have the evidence Darren. Now actions speak louder than words. I stand up with my hands up and move into the lounge. Patrice lays face down on the floor and doesn't move. While you put your gun right in front of yourself. I'll walk towards you and close the door behind me. If you go for the gun Patrice can get away, but I can't. But I know you'll track her down. So I give you something you want. Something to finish this for ever. Bill paid in full and you leave my family alone.'

'I'm listening.'

'When I get to the middle of the room, I'll lay down…' John took a deep breath and swallowed. '…and you can…you can strangle me while Patrice gets away. You won't need to kill my family because you've achieved what you wanted. No more innocent people die. I know you Darren. You're not like this. And this killing…it'll be starting to weigh on you, just like what happened to your family has weighed on me. It gets to be a heavier burden as the years go by Darren. Believe me. You've done what you came to do. My life is…it's screwed Darren…all those people.'

He thought for a long time. 'Okay. But she ties your hands together tight while you're under the gun.'

John looked him in the eye. 'Okay Darren. I stand in front of her, in front of the door, so if you shoot me, she can get away. In which case all bets are off.' The whole thing was a complicated arrangement, and Darren had to have his gun on John while Patrice got some rope, and, in line with the trust arrangement, she had to agree not to call the police because their daughter was in the mix. While she was facing him, trembling as she tied his wrists together, he gave her a strange look. It calmed her. Though she wasn't sure why. Soon John was laying in front of Darren. The Kiwi's gun lying just above his head. It took some fairly strident abuse to get Patrice run while all she could do was cry in confusion.

'You're such a fucking moron Johnny Boy. I could spend hours doing this. Bring you in and out of consciousness. Again and again. It's not pleasant.' Darren moved to clasp John around the neck, a look of hate in his eyes. 'And I'll do what I want to your family. Why should I keep a promise to you, you piece of shit?' He saw John drive his neck forcefully upwards as if he had suddenly realised what a fool he'd been and was going to try to escape. Darren's grasp locked around his neck. It was too late by the time the attacker pulled back, a paralysis was creeping up his arms and then though his body. He fell on his side.

John had used this trick before. In those cases appearing to fail to fend off an attack. Or he used the same drug in gloves he'd made with a dozen small needs in each. He's left them at the farm about which he was annoyed with himself about.

'Who's the moron now Darren.' John was laughing with a rich humour driven, in no small degree, by relief. 'I mean who asks to be strangled? How fucking stupid are you? And what's this Johnny Boy crap. A theatrical crock of shit to make you feel more intelligent? A waste of breath Dazza. There's no cure for the kind of dumbness you have.'

Patrice had not run but had come back through the veranda with a cricket bat. She stopped to take in the revised circumstances. 'Tell me what the fuck's going on John.'

'Christ. Listen Patrice. I'm having a rough night here. You are in the middle of something way, way bigger than you think. But I'm going to sort it out and then there will be plenty of time to provide explanations and make choices. Would you mind untying me.' She did this while trying to catch up with the latest developments.

John started to drag Darren out of the room. By the hair.

She took a deep breath and made her best pretence of reasonableness. 'Fair enough John. Give me something to go on.'

He dropped Darren's head so it made a clunk on the carpet. 'This embarrassment to humanity killed the five innocent people on my patient list and made it look like suicide. Not very well but the investigations were light on because of who those people were. I went to watch over number five for the last few nights however, to my enduring shame, he outsmarted me and knocked me out. And it hurts like hell by the way.' He gave the man on the floor a resounding kick. 'I came to before he could set up everything here how he wanted it.' John was tempted to mention the fact that if she'd run into the bush as he'd asked it might have saved her some trauma. 'He was dumb enough to believe I gave a shit about his family and I would let myself be strangled. Jesus. What a dickhead.' He kicked Darren again. 'So I'm going to deal with him and leave all of the evidence I found at whatever shitty little place he shares with some rats and cockroaches.' John looked down and shook his head. 'You'll be another weirdo trophy hunter.' Another kick was delivered.

She was tentative. 'And they won't find him…alive?'

'That's right Patrice. He's about to come down with a nasty case of deadness.'

'No police?'

'Do you like your life as it is or…or how it's going to be…or fucked up forever because of this person shaped turd.'

Patrice was shaking her head. 'You're…going to kill him….'

'No Patrice. I am eventually going to kill him.' This was a very different John to what she was used to. 'If you believe it's the right thing to contact the police for this…' He kicked Darren in the head. 'At least give me a few hours. He's paying Patrice. For Sunny first, and then right down the line.'

Patrice was quiet for a while. 'Good.' He started to drag Darren out by the hair again, ultimately it was too short, so he went for the collar. 'John.' Her husband smiled across. He heard a tone in her voice he hadn't heard in years. 'I like this version…of you.'

'I'd love to be the real John. For you.' He was smiling. Happy. 'You and I are going to start to have some fun again.' He walked over and swept his wife up like a soldier on VE day and kissed her like he hadn't done for twenty years. He was glad it was finally over.

'Wait for a call from that wayward daughter of yours and be ready for a girls night out. A big one.'

John and Darren were in the commodore driving sedately west. 'You're a bit of lucky charm there Darren. Came along and repaired my marriage. Big thank you for that.' The phone rang. John put it on speaker.

'Senior Detective.'

'Scout Leader Detective. That's right. Big news.'

'You caught the Dice Killer?'

'Nearly as good. The Handymen are being loaded into a paddy wagon as we speak.'

'You followed the Yellow Brick Thumbs at night.'

'We'd started to play with some theories about where they were. However it was the brilliant profiling analysis sent from your e-mail address early this morning, but with the very mysterious 'Hazel wrote this' below the text. She gave us a tight circle of where the killers would be hiding based on their 'penchant for orienteering' and the fact that, the photos of the hands we found, which she somehow got to see, each had a tiny little orchid in the frame. Our Botany Department failed to pick up on that one.'

'The hands might have gone all over, but they were always part of an orchid hunt. And the 'orchid aficionado' would probably be near a good place. And yet they still needed a wifi to overdosed on crime drama streaming binges. Turns out they were operating from in a house near the edge of Ku Ring Gai Chase National Park. Two of them. Both studying to be forensic scientists. They kept the hands, when not on tour, in the freezer compartment in a beer fridge with the beer.'

'Only in Australia Detective. It makes you proud doesn't it.'

'But there's more.'

'How can there be more?'

'The Dice Killer. The DNA was destroyed on the Dice, we think by radiation. But the dots are tattoos. Our boffins have found that in a few places on one of the Dice the ink allowed the cells to leave a kind of shadow in it. I happened to have a file on my desk when the information came in on the Dice DNA. Now that I think of it the singular is Die. Anyhow the DNA report had the same last name as another report on my desk. The person you identified behind a metal door. Sunny Sullivan.'

'I knew Sunny's last name was Sullivan. Were they related.' John sounded interested.

'Uncle. Burned to a crisp in a house fire.'

John sounded concerned Bruxton might be drawing the wrong conclusions. 'I know Sunny couldn't have done it. She found it hard to hold down a job let alone plan a murder and she was genuinely terrified of that man. If someone did that to her uncle, I can't say I'm bothered. She never spoke about him but I read the reports.'

'I think we'll know who the killer is pretty soon John. There's a certain seventeen-year-old profiling genius who's advised me she'll have him collared within days.'

'Ah. Be careful Detective. It might be her. I've always had my suspicions about that girl. She's a wily one and I caught her looking at the files I brought home once when she was fifteen. There could be a twist for you. She told me once she was sick of the patriarchy dominating the serial killer space. Now that she's helped to catch the Handymen, she'll have the credibility to throw you right off course.'

'I'm going to keep a close eye on that girl. She's renamed them the Orchid Killers by the way.'

'How about you come to dinner some time. Surveillance. Our house. Meet Patrice and Hazel.'

'I'd love that. Really love it.'

'I've got to go Senior Detective. Just about to carve somebody into dice.'

Bruxton snorted. 'Don't keep the knife too sharp.'

As they drove along John said. 'Darren do I know you well enough to guess you have certain something I'd find very interesting in the boot.' The paralysed man had been trying to make some kind of noise all through the conversation. John pulled up and got out on the deserted country road. Darren heard a huge 'Yeah.' From the back of the car and watched John return with an esky full of beer and put it in the back next to the man with a sock in his mouth. John drained one in under a minute before opening another one and driving off. They were driving through farmland. 'I'd give you a beer, but you're paralysed and can't drink it. It would dribble out. And you have a sock in your mouth. And don't blame me if you're a victim of your own hygiene issue. Darren Boy? Dazza? You were always such a wanker Darren. You must practice every night to be so good at it.'

The phone rang and he realised he hadn't called his daughter. Before Hazel could say anything, John said. 'Have I told you how beautiful you are and have you heard the news.'

'I haven't heard any news because I've been having panic attacks about why you got me to get out of the house so fast.'

'Sorry about that. You know how I over react to the tiniest little things. You can stand down on the panic. Situation is under control. Except, Dad's kind of busy tonight and, listen carefully; I will pay you, as a one-time offer, a grand not to ask why I'm busy tonight. Ever. The other thing is your mum's ready for you to come and take her out for a girl's night out.'

'Hello. A grand buys my silence. We're in two grand territory for the girls night out thing. And are you drinking. It sounds like your drinking and driving?'

'You remember the little talk we had about parental hypocrisy. I'm surprised I need to repeat myself young lady. But the news. The news Hazel. Is that you cracked the biggest serial killer case of the last few weeks wide open.'

'The killers, the Orchid Killers are receiving as much police brutality as the cops believe they can get away with as we speak.'

'Now that's cool. Though…I hope I haven't given you the impression I'm surprised at all. I want my two grand and a detective badge. A real one. I know Bruxton will do it if I never show it to anyone. But I'm way to humble to ask. So add that to the list. Dice Killer here I come.'

'Okay. We're on a roll Hazel. This is our chance at restore and last piece in the puzzle of family harmony.'

'Father, a thing, in this case family harmony, has to exist before you can restore it. I'm surprised you're not intelligent enough to have figured it out.' John knew, that like him, his daughter was riding a huge wave of relief and simply wanted get all the way to shore by talking shit.

'You were little Hazel. Too young to remember. But here's an important yellow brick in that road. Karaoke Bar. At least half an hour. One Elvis song. Bonus thousand dollars, with the other two. But I want footage.' He would need to solicit a promise to never tell her mother he has handing over three grand. Especially for the last two things.

Her voice became serious. 'I really don't think I can do that dad. Have you heard mum sing. I'm still a little young and delicate child in that singular regard. And family harmony may be a bit of a yawn for me to be truthful. How can I play one of you off against the other and experience the kind of angst and edginess I've become accustomed to if you two…dare I say it; start reconciling each other again.'

'You my dear are heading for that very special niche of theatre known as car salesmanship. Okay. Different deal. Your mother's primed for you to take her out. If you can convince her to buy you booze and you both get totally shit faced you get the grand and a ticket to any concert you want. Interstate travel. Four star. Two nights. One friend. Girl variety.'

'Okay. I can take one for the team and get fucked up for a doomed attempt at family harmony. And the karaoke grand is still on the table if I get so smashed I believe I can cope with it.'

'Get her to launch into The Ghetto, thirty seconds of footage and get the hell out of there. However when you get home to pick her up she might be a little uptight.'

'And?'

'And so lead off with 'Mum I love you so much. Let's go out and get pissed.'

'Okay. By the way this is cash on the barrel. I can't buy drugs and pay gigolos via bank transfers.'

'Text me the evidence. I'm sending your mother a text right after you hang up. Yes. Texting, while driving. While pissed. And you must never, never, never do anything like that Hazel. Ever.'

'After telling me to get the fuck out of the house, what do you think I'm doing right now.' The line went dead.

John looked across and spoke clearly. 'Darren you're a good luck charm. Father. Daughter. Mother reconciled. Crimes solved. Boom. Beer. I'm pretty sure there's a winning lotto ticket in your wallet.' He leaned across to pull the sock out. 'I'm pulling this out so you can tell me how pleased you are for us. In the hope I might go easier on you.' John didn't get any thanks. 'Well fuck you then. And you've helped me decide on our next holiday location. It's beautiful New Zealand. I might say Hi to some of the people I liked. I might say bye to some people I didn't. Like what's left of your family.'

John stopped at an old shed. It was halfway through the process of falling down. He had a very low intensity headlamp on his head and dragged Darren through the cow shit into it. There was a chain block on a length of H section steel bolted to the rafter which was once used to lift motors out of cars. Once the foot deep straw and cow shit was removed, he used the chain block to lift a concrete panel out of the floor of the shed. It revealed a space the size of a large bedroom below. He rolled Darren into the space and there was a thud. 'Oh. Sorry Darren. Forgot to bring the stairs down. Are you're okay?'

He reached in and pulled a rope on a pulley, on the ceiling of the room below, and it lowered the stairs held against the top of the chamber. There was one road in. It had a motion sensing camera at the T junction five kilometres away. Everyone thought John loved having a small herd of cattle though the farmer next door looked after them. They were separate from the dairy heard and he used them beef cattle so they were low maintenance. John left Darren where he was and got onto the computer. 'This stuff doesn't happen by itself Darren. It's a process of continuous improvement. I've been having all kinds of ideas since I realised what you did to Sunny. And how about those fucking tattoo dots.'

'You relax and I'll do some research on the net about some cool new techniques I've been thinking about on the drive in.' He put some headphones on and sat in front of a computer.'

'Darren was starting to feel the effects of the paralysis wear off a little and tried to move one arm and thought he could drag himself around but knew that would be useless. He saw that the bench John was sitting at had things visible protruding over the edge. The uses for which he didn't want to contemplate. Then he saw a knife right under John's chair which must have fallen off some time before. He knew it was a slim chance, but he might as well take it. He dragged himself slowly forward like a lame commando. If he could get the knife and drive into John's calf, remove it quickly and then drive it anywhere in his face when he turned to look down maybe he could wait till whatever he'd been injected with wore off and escape his fate. Or at least slit his own throat. It was agonising, but the paralysis was slowly retreating. John's head was bopping up and down to unheard music in the headphones. As soon as he got a good grasp of the hilt he drew it back and drove it hard into John's calf. But nothing happened. He did it again.

John looked down and laughed and then moved out of the way. 'I love this part. It never gets old Dazza. Silly Johnny Boy leaves a knife on the floor. You hatch a desperate plan. Oh dear. It's a trick knife.' John swoops down and takes the knife from Darren's recovering hand. 'See the mirror there. I watched your every move. And this.' He pushed the blade in and out rapidly. 'Might do some damage to an eyeball. And me doing research Darren? There's no internet in here you fucking idiot.' He put the knife down and clapped his hands together and gave a look of pure excitement. 'Come on Darren. Let's get this party started.' John put handcuffs attached to a collar around Darren's neck and part lifted, part dragged him to a table as he struggled the small amount he was able to. John strapped him to the table with heavy leather straps. Two for each limb and one for the neck and took the temporary restraint off. Once he was held tightly John said. 'Darren. You're special. I'm going to wait a while to make certain the paralysis effect is gone. I've got some packing up to do. We can chat while I work.'

'You remember your sister Darren. Reminds me of my daughter. Not. Of course I wasn't even married back then. Had a beautiful girl waiting for me at home though.'

'Graduated from the University of Sydney and went to New Zealand to work in my dad's mate's practice in Auckland as a junior to get something on my CV. Your sister got referred to us by the Highschool. Depression and anxiety. These days those things aren't mental health problems anymore. You're abnormal if you don't have them. This girl didn't want an appointment. But if she refused to go, that wasn't a good look either. Then she saw an angle. She started to tell me some pretty disturbing things about…was it Tyrone. You're brother. I forget…you had a so many. Oh yeah, but he was your twin brother. Identical twins. And yet you were the one hit by the ugly stick. How is that even possible?'

Darren found he could talk again. He had regained most of his sensation. Which was now a concern. He glared at John. 'That little bitch was just a fucking liar. Tyrone would never do that. She was manipulating you like she did my family and everyone else. Do you have any idea what it's like to lose a twin brother? All because you believed that fucking town bike.'

'I was young Darren, but unlike you I wasn't stupid. I knew you're bother liked to go for a ride. And from what I understood the fucking prick liked rough riding. But even he wouldn't sink as low as that town bike. What a fucking skanky bitch you had for sister. You're family Darren.'

'I mean fuck. How do people get like you. She'd never been in a fancy office and left alone with a man who to her, must have money to burn. And she wanted some.'

Darren went quiet. 'Yes Darren. You're sister decided to fuck me over like she was doing to Tyrone. And why was she doing a number on Tyrone Darren. She didn't care either way about Tyrone you dickhead. She hated you. And now she also threatened to say all kinds of terrible things about me. I could see she would think nothing of destroying my career before I'd really started it. So I started giving her money. To keep her quiet until I sorted out my plan. But we still had an hour a week and so she told me everything in all its gory detail. You people are seriously fucked up. She thought she was manipulating me by getting me to help write a letter with all 'the right words in it'. A bunch of made-up shit about your brother. I made at least half of it up because she was too fucking dumb to even come up with good lies. Even back then Darren, those kind of lies stick like shit to a blanket whether you did anything wrong or not. If someone tells those kinds of lies about you; you're screwed. Your mother disowned him, your father responded by drinking more and you. Where were you Darren? Juvenile detention for selling drugs.'

'Ha. And you were doing that for your older brother who was ripping you off by the way. Tyrone needed his twin brother Darren. Really needed him. But no. So it was Sayonara Tyrone.'

Darren struggled pointlessly against the bonds.

'You're delicate petal of a sister believed the airline ticket I showed her was real. That was back in the day they had tickets. She thought she was going to get the big pile of cash I'd drawn out and showed her in my drawer. I read out a letter I'd written myself from a 'good friend' of mine who was going to help her settle in Sydney. Pictures of the nice house my friend lived in and the dog she had. Photos I downloaded from some random person on the internet. She'd never heard of a thing called a passport Darren. I'd got her believe that trying to blackmail thing was forgiven, and I'd decided to make a project of her. To help her get out of her terrible circumstances. What a dumb bitch. She would probably be stupid enough to believe it if I told her she could strangle me. In her last moments Darren I did share with her the irony that I had manipulated her into writing a letter which she said she she'd met someone who could get her on one of the big boats in the harbour with Panama written on the back and 'get away from the people who have destroyed my life'.'

'And this brings us to one of the many differences between you and me Darren. When I throw someone off a bridge they're cut up and neatly packed into suitcases which I filled up with concrete. Yeah. I didn't drop her head first on a pylon and then leave some of my own fingerprints and her hair on the bridge. You're such a fuckwit.'

'But she'd been talking. Bragging about the dumb fucker of a counsellor she was screwing over and, she said literally screwing. That was bullshit. I didn't go there ...I mean Jesus...who knows what I would catch from tramp like that. Word got back to you I'd helped her write that letter and given her ten grand and a new life in Australia. Why would I give a nasty, manipulative piece of work like that any help. She wanted Tyrone thrown in the can because of what you did. I believed that part you piece of shit. I made a bit of a hash of things that time around. Got involved in a family incest and drug syndicate. Oh.' John looked concerned all of a sudden. 'Whoops. I wasn't supposed to tell you any of that Darren. Patient/Doctor confidentiality. Damn. You won't tell on me will you?' He shook his head. 'The Psychologies Board might take my licence away. Although...I don't even know if there is such a thing Darren you loser.'

John was saying all this as he was casually putting things in boxes in the middle of the room ready for burning.

'My mother killed herself because of you. She was a good woman.'

'From what I heard that was probably true. It wasn't me though. I think she'd had enough of the deadbeats she'd spawned and the pathetic drunk she lived with. I'm surprised she didn't praise me up in a suicide note for bringing her to her senses. There's a silver lining to everything though mate. At least she couldn't breed anymore.' John laughed. This was a side to his personality Patrice, and Hazel and Bruxton would never get to see.

Darren had been looking around the walls. There were neatly painted dice. One for each position up to six. Underneath one to five there were two photos. One of a comparatively young person, and one of someone older. Below that was a small refrigerator with a glass front. Five pink dice with black dots from one to five. Only one side with the dots. John saw him looking around. 'When I got back from New Zealand I decided I thought it would be fun to become one of those Superheroes Americans are so fascinated by. My superpower was going to be to find people I decided were very bad, take them to an underground lab, and torture them.'

'That led to years of meticulous planning. I spent three years just establishing this place. Back then I assumed it would be a passing infatuation I had with a dramatic idea. It was fun leading a secret life and I'll admit Darren there is a small possibility I have a dark site that needs…exercise. Then I started work on a Program. I read the file of a girl called Sunny. Her uncle went first. I had to spread them out. One of the people in the Program turned out to be a pain in the ass so I didn't care so much about his traumatic past. I worry sometimes Darren I've become a tiny bit insensitive.' John laughed. 'Ha. Then I stop worrying about it.' He walked up close to his captive and smiled down at him. 'And here you are again, making everything work out right. Because you're lucky number six. I was worried I wasn't going to be able to finish every side.'

'Don't worry. I can assure you Darren. Everyone here leaves alive. Bit of skin missing. Quite a bit. Among other things. In your case you'll be able to enjoy the gases coming from the burning interior of a shitty old Commodore. I'll only let it burn slowly initially Darren.' John went to the bench to get a wooden box. But he detoured to the wall and pulled off the picture of Sunny. She was a rough diamond. Really rough. But there was a whole lot of diamond.

John walked up to Darren and showed him the picture. 'Remember her Darren. Sunny. Right now you would never believe it is possible for you to regret something so much as killing her.' He smiled. 'I'm pretty good at this now. And I'm in no hurry. This is for her.'

It was a while before Bruxton could get out to dinner at their house. During that time John sterilised and drenched the small room in acid after burning everything. He had clean fill brought out and buried some of the space by hand and then had excavator come in and smash in the slab and backfill the area which filled it with concrete and more fill. He did all this as part of a very generous 'sale' in which the farmer paid a small price as long as John brought everything back to ground level. This involved the excavator smashing up the shed to leave a big pile of wood over the top of where the cellar had been. They had a family evening at the farm, sitting in camp chairs, having to move back several times when the heat got too intense. In accord with the agreement John had a dozer level the ashes. He'd brought in some truckloads of good quality soil and the machine pushed several feet of it over the ash pile, mounding it up to account for any settlement after which he seeded it heavily.

As it was coming into spring, in less than a month the farmer could pull the adjoining fences down and there would be milkers roaming over the place.

Darren was found dead in his car. His veins full of a cocktail of drugs, more of which were found in his small flat. It had a chest with small 'trophies' from each his victims. Sometimes only pictures but a hair sample from Sunny and some possessions of Matty's. The police somehow failed to make a connection between the five victims of the ENZED killer and John. Three more serial killer cases were now being actively investigated. One killer was getting episodes of a new crime drama every week before they went to air on a streaming service so that when the episode came out a murder exactly the same as the one on the episode had been committed the day before in Sydney. Ratings had gone through the roof.

It meant the Dice Killer got very little attention because the Dice were never alluded to in any investigations and the focus of the detectives, influenced by Bruxton and by extension Hazel, moved on to the more sensational cases. They even heard one streaming service was developing a story along the lines of a seventeen-year-old high school girl teaming up with a curmudgeonly detective who cut across the grain. And had few friends.

But now Bruxton had a few. Half way into the second meal he was invited to, those around the table heard. 'That ENZED case Detective Bruxton. It had this…kind of wrinkle in it.' Hazel intoned this authoritatively.

'A wrinkle you say Assistance Detective Hazel.'

'Yes. You know when you're ironing a shirt, especially the arms sometimes and there's this wrinkle and it simply won't go away.'

'Is ironing something you're an authority on…Assistant Detective Hazel.' Ventured Patrice. A month earlier, Hazel had surprised everyone by asking if her mother would like to 'accompany her' to a concert in Melbourne. Patrice could not be more delighted and there was a tacit understanding that once a year mother and daughter were going to go on a trip together and get 'totally fucked up'. It created a balance Patrice worked hard to develop with the other two offspring. No one came close to the bond she formed with Hazel though.

Hazel put the back of her hand on her forehead with theatrical exhaustion at what she was called upon to forbear. 'Idiom sprinkled with irony. Esteemed mother. If I may continue. The Dice Killer, and the ENZED Killer. Connected via happenstance. I think not.'

'I must get out and buy that dictionary.' Said the senior of a very successful, but low-key partnership.

'Intersection esteemed curmudgeon.'

'What is it with this family and big words.'

'I can see something at that intersection. It's…it's crystal clear in my young, still quickening mind.'

'Oh.' Said Bruxton. 'An…intersection you say.'

'What I see at the intersection, with remarkable clarity, is a late model sedan. I can't quite see the make but it's nice. Deep blue. Tinted windows. Inside there's a carefree young woman with her latest…squeeze. She tries not to learn their names. She's pondering. There's an offer from a Broadway theatre company to consider. However there's the vital services she provides to the wider society as a serial killer profiler. To follow the latter path would mean rejecting the celebrity that said society would lavish upon her. The lights at the intersection change, she drives through it. Who knows what her inscrutable mind will settle upon. The enlightenment of the masses via theatre is also no small contribution to the human condition.'

Those sitting around all pretended to be bemused and nonplussed at the excursion into car imaginings.

'However...' The girl on the cusp of getting her P Plates continued. 'If I was a mere pedestrian. Having stumbled upon that intersection. My circumstances might cause me to look more closely.' She made a steeple with her fingers and looked at the ceiling. 'At the wrinkle.'

'It sounds to me me...' John was authoritative now. 'You need something colloquially known as...a job.' Hazel now composed a face of surprise at the unlikely suggestion. John looked at Patrice. 'And...we'll need to negotiate the definition of 'late model'.'

It was a pleasant meal. They made sure Bruxton knew they hoped there would be many more.

Patrice and John were sitting on the veranda looking out at the bush. She pulled out the phone John hadn't seen since it hit him in the head. 'I found this in the drawer. Wasn't quite sure what to do with it. Then I realised that it's your phone and your business. But...' Patrice's voice held a note of sorrow. 'I wanted to see her again and also let you know this had arrived in the afternoon before we had our little 'talk'.' She handed it over.

Sunny and Jess were pictured not long after John had seen her for the last time. They were both smiling in a selfie, an arm around each other's shoulder. The text under the photo read. Mates again. Thanks for your advice Doctor J.

He looked at it for a long time and said. 'Thanks.'

www.ingramcontent.com/pod-product-compliance
Lightning Source LLC
Chambersburg PA
CBHW051418170626
46809CB00006B/2214